His voice was a... with tender concern

"Do you think it might help to talk about this fellow who seems to have put you off men for life?" Ran inquired gently.

Rena's thoughts were a jumble. Tell *him* about it? But wasn't that what she'd been wanting to do for two long years?

"All right," she said. "He met me; he seduced me; he left me. That's about all there is to it."

"Presumably he was the first...and the last man you've been to bed with," he said with astonishing accuracy. "I suppose he must have told you he loved you. I've never done that just to get a woman into my bed."

Liar! The word screamed in her mind.

"But love," he added, "isn't the only reason two people go to bed together."

Books by Victoria Gordon

HARLEQUIN ROMANCES

2427—THE SUGAR DRAGON
2433—WOLF AT THE DOOR
2438—THE EVERYWHERE MAN
2458—DREAM HOUSE
2469—ALWAYS THE BOSS
2531—DINNER AT WYATT'S
2540—BATTLE OF WILLS

These books may be available at your local bookseller.

For a free catalog listing all titles currently available,
send your name and address to:

Harlequin Reader Service
P.O. Box 52040, Phoenix, AZ 85072-2040
Canadian address: Stratford, Ontario N5A 6W2

VICTORIA GORDON

blind man's buff

Harlequin Books

TORONTO • NEW YORK • LONDON
AMSTERDAM • PARIS • SYDNEY • HAMBURG
STOCKHOLM • ATHENS • TOKYO • MILAN

Harlequin Presents first edition May 1984
ISBN 0-373-10689-0

Original hardcover edition published in 1982
by Mills & Boon Limited

Copyright © 1982 by Victoria Gordon. All rights reserved.
Philippine copyright 1982. Australian copyright 1982.
Except for use in any review, the reproduction or utilization of
this work in whole or in part in any form by any electronic,
mechanical or other means, now known or hereafter invented,
including xerography, photocopying and recording, or in any
information storage or retrieval system, is forbidden without
the permission of the publisher, Harlequin Enterprises Limited,
225 Duncan Mill Road, Don Mills, Ontario, Canada M3B 3K9.

All the characters in this book have no existence outside the
imagination of the author and have no relation whatsoever to
anyone bearing the same name or names. They are not even
distantly inspired by any individual known or unknown to the
author, and all the incidents are pure invention.

The Harlequin trademarks, consisting of the words
HARLEQUIN PRESENTS and the portrayal of a Harlequin,
are trademarks of Harlequin Enterprises Limited and are
registered in the Canada Trade Marks Office; the portrayal
of a Harlequin is registered in the United States Patent
and Trademark Office.

Printed in U.S.A.

CHAPTER ONE

THERE was no footpath along Walker Street where it separated the college from the southern edge of the showgrounds. And not the best of street lighting, either, thought Rena as she stumbled for the second time since putting the bright lights of the college entrance driveway behind her.

Ahead of her, the road dipped slowly towards the creek that formed the western boundary of the college grounds, and most of the houses on her left were as dark as the night around her. The headlights of the oncoming traffic were more hindrance than help, blinding in their intensity, and she cursed idly as she stumbled yet a third time while crossing the rutted driveway to one of the darkened houses.

'Item one: remember to bring a torch next week,' she told herself, and then smiled, nodding her head like a perky robin in pleasure at the thought. It was, she realised, one of the first occasions in two long years when she had actually begun to plan ahead, to begin the evolvement from the day-to-day existence she had been living.

Perhaps, she thought, it was an omen. Perhaps taking this creative writing course was the right thing to do, the first real step towards a more normal existence. Perhaps . . .

Certainly her songwriting hadn't helped. Not, at least, in the one area that really mattered—getting Ran Logan out of her mind, out of her past as well as her future. Maybe she could do it with prose.

'You could do it easily if you weren't such a sensitive, gullible fool,' she told herself aloud, wincing visibly at the truth of her own words. Even with two years and nearly a thousand miles between them, Randall Logan had the devilish power to stride into her mind without warning and fiendishly kick apart her every attempt to put her life back in order.

He was ever there. In the poetry of her songs—songs that her audiences seemed to love for their poignant, passionate, heartrending honesty—it was his eyes and his voice that tugged at her heart-strings as she sang. When the words and rhythm of the poetry formed in her mind during the long hours of almost nightly sleeplessness, it was his touch, his very essence that turned pleasant, happy melodies into tragic epics of lost love and ruined virtue.

Rena wondered as she neared her destination, the old wood-frame building called the 'staff house', if somehow this writing course might help her to sort out her feelings for once and all, to put her hurt and her disillusionment into proper perspective, to help herself live again.

It had been a spur-of-the-moment decision to take the course. She had paid little attention to the advertisement in that morning's newspaper, yet somehow the title "creative writing" had seemed to leap from the page, clawing at her awareness. A telephone call from work had provided the rest: she could enrol that evening during the first of the ten weekly lessons, then sort out the paperwork later.

She stepped ahead more quickly as the bright lights of the staff house beckoned, lighting her way through the vehicle gate and round to the front entry, where narrow steps led up to a wide verandah and the bright-lit hallway leading from it.

Rows of student desks—each of them little more than a stool with attached folding table—filled the large

double room on her left, and Rena guessed it must
originally have been the lounge-dining room of the
house.

Trying to shield her eyes until they adjusted to the
harsh fluorescent lighting, she paused in the doorway,
aware of half a dozen people already seated and two,
perhaps three more walking up the hallway behind her.
Not an overly large class, she thought, and was grateful
for that. In truth she had no idea what to expect of the
class, but certainly smaller numbers would allow more
room for individual attention from the instructor.

Flickering her long eyelashes in a final bid to
adjust to the lighting, she stepped forward a single
pace. Then her gaze fixed in wide-eyed shock on the
figure behind the large table at the front of the room
and she halted, fixed to the floor as if glued. A great
shiver rippled through her body and she choked back
the sudden upsurge of bile that rose bitter in her
throat.

Ran Logan! It couldn't be—but it was! Rena didn't
need her astounded eyes to tell her the truth of it; her
body fairly screamed recognition, tingling with the
memories she had been so vainly trying to throttle
these past two years.

'It can't be!' Some elfin voice in her mind screamed
the phrase over and over and over in an endless litany
so loud she feared she had also screamed it. But it was
. . . it was . . .

Ran Logan! That same unruly mane of hair, hair the
colour of milk chocolate and the texture, she knew only
too well, of soft copper wire. That same prominent,
slightly crooked nose, with flaring nostrils above a
wide, sensuous mouth—a mouth that could evoke
heaven with its touch . . . or sheer desperation with its
words. And behind the reflective lenses of the sunglasses he wore, Rena knew, were those unique,

copper-hued eyes, deepset but alive to every nuance of human behaviour.

Eyes that at this moment were fixed upon her! Rena wanted to scream, to run . . . fleeing both present and past before it engulfed her in renewed pain and agony. She wanted to disappear, to faint, even to die. Anything—so long as it meant escape.

But she couldn't move. Even when those behind her lost their patience and gently began to prod at her, she couldn't take a single step either backward or forward. Her own eyes were welded to the shimmering surface of those sunglasses; her feet as firmly welded to the wooden floor beneath them.

Would he speak? Could he *dare* to speak, after what he'd done? He could, Rena knew. Ran Logan would dare the devil himself should it suit his purpose. But could she answer? She doubted it. She was a statue, no longer alive, no longer warm and breathing but only a pillar of ice as cold as the heart within her.

'Are you going in, or what?' a feminine voice hissed in Rena's ear, hoarse with impatience and barely audible. But it was loud enough. Ran Logan's head lifted slightly, his nostrils trembling like those of a spirited stallion.

Then he spoke, his voice that once-loved, melodious deep voice that could—and did—bring goosebumps to Rena's bare arms. It rumbled like the drums in some hidden, forbidden jungle, like the surf on a lonely beach, like the thunder of her own terrified heart. Only louder.

'Please come in and take a seat,' he said. 'I may not be able to see, but I assure you I don't bite or anything, and my . . . blindness isn't contagious.'

Blind! Rena stood in shocked disbelief, oblivious now to the growing impatience of those behind her. Her dark blue eyes searched across the room, seeking the lie but finding only the reflected disguise of the sunglass lenses and then, suddenly, the ivory whiteness of the walking stick propped beside his long, muscular legs.

'Come on!' A not-so-gentle nudge almost sent her flying off balance into the room, but Rena caught herself in time to twist aside so that she landed instead in the nearest empty seat.

Blind? But how? When? What had happened? The questions scurried like mice, nibbling at the fringes of her concentration and diffusing her ability to comprehend.

It couldn't be true. And yet it must be. He had looked directly at her, but without the tiniest hint of recognition. And not even Ran Logan could be that cold . . . that callous. He simply couldn't fail to recognise her.

Or could he? Rena thought hard, focussing her mind on the picture of herself she had skimmed over in the mirror before embarking from her small flat earlier that evening.

A great long mane of sable hair, not the tight-fitting cap of two years earlier, but now a flowing tide, worn loose and casually . . . no make-up, or at least none by comparison to that she had worn when singing in Sydney as Catherine Conley, but Ran had seen her without make-up—on one too many mornings . . . slimmer? Much, she decided. The slender but shapely twenty-year-old was now a bone-thin woman of twenty-two, but she still didn't *look* all that different.

She had the same dark blue eyes, topped by thick, down-sloping eyebrows and fringed by enormously long lashes. The same tidy nose, neither long nor snub but just right for her face, the same soft, vulnerable mouth and firm but not overly defiant chin. Only the shadows were different—those beneath her eyes now were permanent reminders of poor sleeping, not just

the occasional late night. And those below her cheek-
bones now existed because her cheeks were slimmer,
less full, less youthful.

Her eyes swam back into focus. Ran seemed still to
be looking at her, but she realised then that he was
looking at everyone and no one, his coppery eyes
hidden behind the reflective lenses and only his other
senses at work.

He wore a turtle-necked silken jersey beneath the
light, well-cut sports jacket, and around his neck
gleamed the chain of a medallion hidden in a fold of
shadow. Then he moved—and she had to still a gasp
of amazement.

It couldn't be! (God, she thought, could her mind
say nothing else?) But it was. Rena knew that medallion—intimately. It had been she who chose it, she who
bought it, paid for it with her own money, she who
had first hung it round his strong neck, sealed its arrival with a kiss. It was a wafer of silver on a silver
chain, a wafer imprinted with the month of July. Only
the fourth, a Saturday that year, had been punched
out and replaced with a tiny sapphire.

It was, he'd told her half-jokingly, an engagement
ring for him. Hers, he had said, was being made. Rena,
fool that she was, had even believed him. Diamonds
and sapphires, he had promised—the diamonds for
tradition and the sapphires because that was her
birthstone. She was a Virgo, although only just, with
her birthday on September the twenty-third.

And not even that, any more. Virgo . . . the virgin—
but no more. Not since the day his medallion
honoured, the day she had given him what no diamond,
no sapphire could replace.

Rena shivered, feeling the white froth of hatred as it
seared up from somewhere inside her. She had traded
her virginity for deceit and lies and abandonment—

and now this ... this *bastard* wore the rest of her gift like a badge of triumph, a visible, tangible announcement to the world of how he had misled and deceived her!

She trembled, fingers clenched into fists so tight her long nails drew blood from her palms. And her eyes burned out her hatred to a man who could no longer see it.

Her mind, however, was less able to fixate itself. Instead of a singular, undiluted approach to the situation, it seethed and frothed and foamed with unanswered questions. What was Randall Logan doing here, here in this small provincial Queensland city so far from his Sydney base? How had he been blinded? What in the name of heaven was he doing teaching creative writing on a one-night-a-week basis?

He was famous. He had *been* famous, although perhaps less so, when she had known him. One of the nation's top journalists, then, working in the combined media of radio, television and print and considered the fastest-rising media personality in Australia.

And now ... since his blinding? she wondered ... he was even more famous for his critical, incisive personality profiles, and yet again more for his books. There had been only two and Rena had forced herself to read them both, hoping for some internal effect, some physical or psychic purging of her own wounded soul ...

'... perhaps wondering how I can effect to teach creative writing without being able to read,' he was saying, 'and I won't pretend it will be easy. To be honest, I've never attempted such a thing, not even when I could see. Indeed I'm not a teacher at all; I'm a writer—a working journalist with nigh on twenty years' experience and now a relatively successful novelist. I write for money.'

He paused, then, and once again Rena had the inexplicable sensation that he was looking at her. Worse, that he was actually seeing her. But he couldn't be.

'Not all of you will be here with that in mind,' he continued. 'Indeed, some of you, I suspect, don't know why you're here in the first place. So let us understand each other right from the start.'

Understand each other? Oh, I understand, Rena thought. I understand only too well.

'I can't teach you to write. Nobody can teach you to write except you yourselves,' he said. 'This isn't a basic course in English grammar, nor is it some airy-fairy course for the appreciation of English literature.'

He paused, as much for effect, she suspected, as to allow the murmur of surprise to ripple across the room and then subside.

'I'm presuming you're here because you want to write. I honestly hope most of you have already tried, in which case I guess it's more correct to say you want to write better. Well, there's only one way to do it. You learn to write by writing.'

Another pause. He was, Rena noticed, playing his audience with all the skill of a dedicated fly-fisherman. And he was succeeding. Even without his vision, he was totally attuned to the sounds and the feelings of the ten people in the room. Including . . . her?

·'Some of you won't finish this course.' Was there that oh-so-familiar hint of a sneer on his upper lip? And did he realise it was there? His mouth quirked as if in answer to her silent question.

'It could be as many as half, I estimate. And those who do finish will more than likely hate my guts by the time we're done.'

One of us already does, Rena thought, and immediately twisted in her seat, wondering who might have heard her; the thought had been so clear, so vivid, she feared she had spoken it aloud.

'But personally,' that velvet voice continued, 'to quote one of the most famous of fictional characters—I don't give a damn.'

There were titters at that, and the predictable voices, one whispering and the other loud enough to be heard by all: *Rhett Butler—Gone with the Wind.*

And you forgot the *frankly, my dear*, Rena thought, but then you wouldn't know the meaning of the word, either. Now that the initial shock was over, other parts of her mind were returning to life ... most obviously the voice of survival crying: 'Get out!'

Ran Logan didn't so much as smile. If anything, he looked more sombre, the planes and angles of his face harsh in the vivid lighting. He's thinner, Rena thought. Thinner and ... harder? Not ... physically hungry, but that emaciated, tired sort of hungry you see on the faces of Asian refugees.

Soul-hungry! The word leapt to mind even with the built-in denial. How could he be? He hadn't got a soul. But she wished he would take off the reflective glasses so that she could see his eyes. Were they empty now? Or still alive with their depths of dark, old-copper colouring?

'Get out!' The survival voice was screaming, now, raging against the bastions of curiosity, hatred, anger and agony. She should obey it, she knew that, but cursed herself for a masochist and stayed in her seat.

'There's an element of masochism to all forms of writing, I think,' Ran said then, and Rena shivered again. Another omen? Or just her conscience thrashing about aimlessly?

He didn't wait to let her find out. 'Because rejection is almost as much a part of the game as the writing itself,' he continued. 'For every successful writer, in any genre, there are dozens, perhaps hundreds, who never make the grade. Most never would, but there is a percentage who are simply too sensitive; they couldn't take the criticism, couldn't handle the rejection.'

Oh, I know all about that, Rena sighed to herself—and already was on the verge of listening to that survival voice. Certainly *she* couldn't handle the rejection. Two years . . . and still she hurt at so much as the thought of his betrayal, his rejection of her!

'Now I don't know . . . yet . . . if any of you are near to selling what you write,' he went on. 'Perhaps none of you. I imagine there may even be one or two who wouldn't dream of writing for money, and I have no argument with that philosophy. I don't care why you write—so long as you do it. And at the risk of embarking upon a chicken-or-egg argument, I will simply suggest that without a reader . . . or readers . . . there simply *is* no writing. If you're the only person who's going to read what you write, why bother? You might as well talk to yourself; it's easier.'

There was a murmur, a thin, trailing thread of sound that ran muted through the audience and died as Ran held up his hand.

Rena wasn't surprised. Far from it; she knew only too well the commanding, dominating power of his personality.

'I know,' he said. 'Somebody is going to say that writing helps to clarify their thinking, helps them to truly portray their feelings in a way that thought can't. Perhaps that's true; I hope it is. But to that person I suggest that there *is* a reader—yourself! Because I honestly hope that if you're going to such extremes to clarify your thinking, then you'll read what you write—not only once, but again and again. And that you'll rewrite it, because that will help clarify things even more.'

He smiled then, but it wasn't the old Ran smiling. There was no humour in the gesture, Rena thought. Only a wry, tattered bitterness. Like his two books. However brilliant they might have been, and she tried honestly to believe they were quite brilliant, they too had been steeped in bitterness; they had reeked, she suddenly realised, of cynicism and pain and anger and even rejection.

His blindness? It must have been. She could imagine no woman, no normal human being, with the power or ability to hurt Ran Logan very much at all. And certainly not herself, much as she dearly wished she could.

'Writing,' he said, 'is easy. Rewriting is the hard part of being a writer, because it means going back over things that are important, reliving old mistakes. None of us likes to do that, I suspect, but a professional writer must!'

Then I'm halfway there already, Rena thought, tasting the acid of her own two-year-old bitterness. More than halfway. She had done, it seemed, little else during the past two years but review her mistakes, and the biggest one of all had been her involvement with Randall Logan.

She watched as he lifted a hand, almost wearily it seemed, and touched his brow above the rim of the sunglasses. Long, slender fingers, the fingers of an artist, she had once thought, probed lightly at the lock of hair that had fallen across his forehead.

The Adam's apple below his determined, uncleft chin bobbed slightly as he swallowed, and Rena's eyes widened in honest surprise.

He's nervous, she thought—and nearly shook her head in astonishment. Ran Logan . . . nervous? It was beyond her comprehension. How could he possibly be nervous in front of this audience, when he'd faced

many far larger and more astute so many times in the
past?

'. . . so that's going to be the procedure during the
next ten weeks,' he was saying. 'I shall be doing everything in my power to make you write, and rewrite, and
rewrite again. I shall criticise unmercifully and, some
of you will say, unfairly. You won't like me for it.'

Too right, Rena thought. And me most of all, because I've got a head start. I already know about you
being without mercy . . . without fairness.

He was speaking again, this time discussing writing
in general, but Rena didn't listen. Her mind was two
years in the past, reliving poignant memories, wallowing in pain . . .

They had first met at the small tavern where she
had been singing three nights a week; Ran had been
with another girl, but he had known a friend of a friend
who was sitting alone at a corner table, drinking too
much and obviously lost in the folk songs of Catherine
Conley. Poor Dick had been a regular fan since a bust-
up with his girl-friend, and Rena had allowed her
compassion to express itself in her singing.

When she made to leave him in the company of his
new companions during her first break, Dick had
noisily insisted on her joining them.

And that was my first mistake, she thought. The
first of many. Ran had been dressed that evening in
casual but expensive clothing, a dark shirt open at the
throat and darker trousers over gleaming boots. He had
been polite and silently apologetic for Dick's noisy
behaviour, and before Rena's next break he had hustled
Dick out of the place.

But on her next evening, he had come in alone, this
time dressed for evening and stunningly handsome.
She had looked up at his entrance and immediately
been captured by those deep, dark-copper eyes. A

casual, studied nod as he seated himself near the stage, but no invitation later—as she had half expected and been ready to refuse—for her to join him.

That, she had decided, was surprising, although now she knew it for no more than the carefully-planned gambit it had really been.

Of course she had known who he was. Impossible not to, with his face on television almost daily and his voice a common sound on radio each morning. He arrived again on her next singing night, making her wonder at the time if he had merely selected the tavern as a convenient place to drink without being bothered. Again, he merely nodded, but Rena had been conscious throughout her performance of his eyes upon her.

Being stared at didn't usually bother her. She knew she was attractive, couldn't honestly discount the added attraction of clothing personally selected to match her performance.

She was a folk singer. Not a great one, perhaps not even all that good, she often thought. But she had a rich, rather husky contralto voice and a genuine love for the historic songs she sang in addition to the ones she wrote herself and sometimes included.

Not for her the grubby jeans and unwashed hair which many of her contemporaries favoured. Rena, as Catherine Conley, wore her dark hair short and close to her head, and her clothing—most of it made by herself—was inclined to the peasant necklines or Victorian fullness that suited her. Sometimes she even wore full-sleeved blouses and velvet jerkins, reminiscent of a female Robin Hood.

The evening of Ran's third visit marked the end of a long, arduous day in her regular job as a legal secretary, and that, combined with an unusually quiet and receptive crowd, set a melancholy mood which Rena matched with her music as best she could.

Slow music, soft music, haunting melodies and tragic ballads—her speciality, really, but on that evening it all seemed unusually suitable. And throughout, Randall Logan's coppery eyes, not aggressively undressing her, not even seeking her attention, really. But drinking her mood, somehow supporting her, like the shoulder of an old and trusted friend.

It was an evening without thunderous applause, but that didn't bother Rena. She could tell when her audience was really appreciating her efforts, and this was one such occasion, despite the almost haunting silence that met the end of her efforts.

And somehow, when her first break came and Ran beckoned graciously towards the extra chair at his table, it had seemed so easy, so natural, to accept his invitation. They had talked little, and then about only innocuous subjects, but in his expert manner he had subtly drawn her out, finding out much about her without really offering a great deal of information about himself.

He had been . . . gallant, she had decided later, after he had driven her home and ventured his goodnight with nothing more aggressive than a continental touch of his lips on her fingertips. Gallant . . . and so incredibly comfortable to be with.

Gallant! Rena looked up from her reverie and blasted him with her eyes. Cunning was more like it, she told herself. Cunning and devious and sneaky and oh, so clever.

She glanced round the room, for the first time bothering to evaluate her fellow students. No one noticed; they were all too entranced by their instructor's words, it seemed.

Not surprising. His voice rolled through the room like far-off thunder, soft, but oh, so powerful. Magnetic. To Rena, that voice had been one of Ran's greatest attractions, from the very beginning. Even now it held elements of that initial hypnotic quality, not only for her but for the rest of the class.

They were an unusual mixture, although perhaps not for a class of this type, she thought. A matched pair of students, both in jeans and T-shirts and thongs; a tall, older, grey-haired man who looked like a retired public servant; three women in their late thirties or early forties; and two women and a man in her own age group.

The three older women all appeared to be married; at least they all wore rings on the appropriate fingers and two of them wore that almost indefinable look of a housewife-frump concealing an individual screaming for release. Of the two her own age, Rena judged one to be a serious, studious type, while the other seemed much more flamboyant and outgoing. The younger man, she judged, was about twenty-five, bearded, and apart from the motorcycle helmet beside his chair, not particularly noticeable at all.

Rena wondered how Ran intended to organise his class. Unable to read, would he expect them to recite their work aloud? It seemed a bit much, even with his skilled and highly-trained journalist's memory, to expect to evaluate material on only one hearing.

Could this be why he appeared just that little bit nervous? Was he feeling somewhat out of his depth? Rena sniggered to herself; she hoped he was well and truly beyond his depth, so far beyond that he'd end up making a complete fool of himself.

'. . . let's get this show on the road,' he was saying, his voice altered just enough to command instant attention even from Rena. 'How many of you have ever written anything and actually sold it?'

Silence. Ran nodded slowly and Rena guessed he had expected the lack of response. She herself had lied in her reply—or lack of it. Several of her songs had been published, both as lyrics to other musicians' music and with her own music written for them.

'How many have written anything and tried to sell it?' he asked next. Three hands shot up, Rena's among them, and after a moment's silence there was a murmur of embarrassed giggles as each respondent realised what they had done.

'Marvellously observant lot, aren't you?' Ran asked sarcastically. 'Ever occur to any of you that you've just given me one reason you're having trouble getting published?'

Rena's face was crimson with embarrassment, but she noticed the flamboyant girl her own age, a tall, lithe redhead, only looked angry at the rebuke. The serious-looking one, third among those who had replied so ludicrously, merely shook her close-cropped blonde head as if rebuking herself.

The silence continued as Ran allowed his sarcasm to sink in, and when he finally spoke again it was in a voice brimming with subdued bitterness.

'Now that we've all had our little chuckle, perhaps one of you might be kind enough to *tell* me the answer,' he snapped.

'Three,' replied the redhead with equal venom. 'And I think you're making a bit much of a perfectly reasonable mistake.' She was, Rena decided, not amused.

And neither was Ran, although to those others, not knowing him as she did, his gurgling chuckle must have sounded friendly enough. Had any of them appeared with him on one of his hard-hitting interview programmes, Rena knew, they'd have had sense enough to detect the warning note in that chuckle, like the shaking of a rattlesnake's tail.

Certainly the redhead didn't realise it, Rena noticed. She had obviously taken the chuckle as a sign of friendliness and was even visibly preening at having been noticed.

'A *bit* much,' Ran said in a voice like silk. 'Perhaps. But in future I'd suggest you only hold up your hand if you want to leave the room.'

The class erupted in a chorus of snickers and giggles, none of them too friendly to the recipient of his barbed remark. And this time the redhead's angry flush was obvious to all. She held her tongue, wisely, Rena thought, but the angry swishing of stocking-clad, shapely legs being crossed and recrossed was loud in the hollow silence of the room.

'And how many of you have written anything at all?' he asked, no sign on his face that he was aware of the redhead's discomfort. The reply was a confusing chorus of 'I' and 'Me' mingled with laughter as two hands were raised in opposite corners, only to disappear as quickly as they'd gone up.

Ran chuckled more loudly, this time, and Rena, knowing him, could tell he was honestly amused and not readying another barbed remark.

'That's nine ... out of ten,' she barked in the first bit of silence that occurred, then sat open-mouthed in surprise. Why did I do that? she wondered, even as he replied with a soft-spoken thank-you.

'And are you one of the nine ... or the odd ... woman out?' he asked in that sensuous, silky voice, that voice which still had the ability to send tendrils of desire spurting through her.

Rena paused, confused by her physical reaction as much as by the question. Her mind seemed to have slipped into neutral, and she looked round the room almost in a panic, trying to remember if she had counted herself in the original tally or not.

One of the three older women smiled understandingly and silently raised her hand, flashing bright eyes around the room as she urged the others to follow suit. The gestures were silent, but Rena felt positive Ran realised what was happening; he had that hint of a smirk on his lips.

All hands were up except that of the redhead, who sat glaring, her eyes flashing from Rena to Ran and back again. It was as if she were daring Rena to count her falsely.

Rena had to think; she was totally confused now, and yet surely the redhead had been one of the three to answer his earlier question? Yes!

'Well?' Ran's voice was harsh now, slightly impatient. Obviously he felt the game had gone on long enough. 'What's the matter?' he asked testily. 'Have you run out of fingers?'

Rena gasped. What a horrible question for a man who couldn't see! What if, by some chance, she were an amputee? Surely one already incapacitated—as he was—should know better than to risk such cruelty.

'That was a thoughtless remark. What if you'd found she *didn't* have enough fingers? Or don't insults between cripples matter?'

The redhead! And if Ran's question had been sarcastically thoughtless, what of her own? Surely it had been coldly, deliberately hurtful.

'If she had been . . . crippled, I imagine she'd have been used to such . . . thoughtless remarks,' he replied slowly. And Rena could see the vein in his throat vibrating as he fought to keep his temper. 'Cruelty from others is part of life for people who are incapacitated in one form or another,' he said. 'Still, I take your point and I apologise in hopes it will be accepted.'

'Certainly,' said Rena, now anxious only to have it over. 'And I must, as well. It seems the correct answer is ten out of ten.'

There was silence then, a silence in which he seemed

to look up, stare directly at her. She could feel his gaze despite her knowledge that he could not see. His nostrils flared; she almost imagined she could see his ears quivering.

Rena shrank into her seat, eyes wide as she returned his stare. Could he see? Was this all some ghastly charade . . .some evil, cruel game in which she was but a pawn? Suddenly she was terrified, but as quickly as the emotion struck her Ran turned away without a word or gesture to reveal his true intent.

Perhaps, she thought, he had only been waiting for the redhead to apologise. That must have been it. He had perhaps appeared to be looking at Rena herself, but in reality his ear had been cocked towards where the redhead was sitting.

She hoped! Meanwhile, her survival voice was once again screaming at her to get out, to flee before she found herself involved in something she would not, could not cope with.

Ran now appeared merely thoughtful, but virtually everyone else in the room was staring pointedly at the redhead, who could not be oblivious to such attention.

'Perhaps . . . perhaps I should also apologise,' the woman began. 'It's just that . . . I . . .'

'I think it's clear enough,' Ran interrupted. 'But don't bother to apologise; you'll likely think worse of me than that before this course is over.'

His face betrayed no sign of it, but Rena knew. He was horribly, disturbingly bitter. And angry. Had the redhead's criticism cut more deeply than even Rena herself had guessed? It was, she decided, just possible. She smiled, knowing he couldn't see the smile. And an instant later she was equally glad he couldn't see the guilt that wiped away the smile as if it had never been.

She felt ashamed of herself, to laugh at another's afflictions. No matter how much she knew he deserved that ... and worse, it would not be him she had hurt by such thoughts but herself.

Vengeance is such a petty, useless emotion, she thought. Even fulfilled it could not be satisfying, could provide no sense of completeness. Not for her. And yet ... she longed for some way to repay him for his betrayal, some way to make him suffer as she had. And to hell with fulfilment!

'What we'll do, I think, is something to ensure that each of you during the next week does some writing,' said Ran. 'Not too much, because I realise some of you might not be as quick as others. Is there anyone, by the way, who can't type?'

There was a moment's silence before a single voice piped up. 'I can't ... not very well, anyway.' One of the unisex couple. The female half, which Rena found rather surprising.

Ran, of course, had no such visual assistance to his assessment. His reply was brutally swift and simple. 'Learn!'

And without waiting for any response, argumentative or otherwise, he reached out one long-fingered hand and drew his briefcase towards him.

'I'd like you all to take five minutes now and just write down a few facts about yourselves,' he said. 'Nothing too complicated ... just name, age, marital status if it's relevant, what you do for a living, what kind of writing you've done, or want to do, what interests you, sports, hobbies ... that sort of thing.'

And one eyebrow cocked mischievously above the rim of his sunglasses before he continued, 'Of course I don't have to ask if you've all brought something to write with ... and on?'

Again the silence, this time punctuated by a hiss from her boy-friend before the student piped up again.

'I haven't,' she said, and Ran's lip curled in ill-disguised scorn.

'Then isn't it handy that I have?' he asked, drawing a pad of paper and several pencils from his case. His voice was brutally mocking.

Strike two, thought Rena, and wondered idly if the girl would be returning the next week. Somehow she rather doubted it, unless young love could stand the wrath of Ran's scorn and bitterness.

She wrote quickly, yet cautiously: Rena Collins, twenty-two, secretary, written some poetry, would like to try short stories, perhaps a novel. I like most forms of writing, especially science fantasy, thrillers, good old-fashioned murder mysteries, even romances.

And she stopped. Ought she mention her song-writing? No . . . definitely not. And her marital status, she determined, was none of his damned business. Then she looked down at her own handwriting—rounded, open, rather childish, she thought—and almost laughed.

What was she writing anything for? She certainly wouldn't be there next week anyway. The poor, embarrassed young girl student, busily scribbling away with her borrowed materials . . . she might return. But would Rena? It was beyond logic.

She looked up to find Ran apparently looking at her once more, and so real was the illusion that Rena had to look away, shrinking into her seat so that she was partially hidden by the tall, older man seated ahead of her.

I can't possibly come back, she thought. It would be no more than ten weeks of blatant masochism. Torture.

Ran reached into his briefcase again, this time emerging with a small cassette recorder which he turned over and over in his agile fingers as he waited for his ears to tell him the writing exercise was nearly finished. Finally, it was.

'All right,' he said then. 'What I'd like now is for each of you to come up, one at a time if you please, and read what you've written on to this tape for me. And please don't be shy; by next week I'll be fairly good at matching names to voices, and before the course is over I'll have no problems that way at all.'

He paused, a smile ghosting across his lips. It was the kind of secret smile Rena remembered only too well. 'I'm very good on voices,' he said then, and he was looking at *her*!

CHAPTER TWO

RENA couldn't move. She could hardly, for that matter, so much as draw breath. Gone were the sounds of the other people in the room, drowned by the surging roar of her heartbeat as it echoed in her ears.

Ran reached up then, tugging away the sunglasses and gently massaging with his fingers at the bridge of his nose and along his heavy eyelids. He was still *looking* towards Rena, and for the first time she was able to actually see his eyes.

They were the same! The same dark copper colour that she knew could shift even darker or flood with light to the shade of a new penny when he was aroused. And yet they were different, too. Something was missing, some essence, some element of life. Ran was looking towards her, but his eyes were unfocused; he clearly didn't see her, didn't see anything.

Blind! And for the first time the truth of it seeped into her brain. In doing so, it bypassed the coals of hatred, the banked furnace of her own pain, and a flood of compassion welled up inside her, almost bringing tears with it.

One thing to wish revenge, to wish him hurt for what he'd done to her. But this! No, she decided, not *this* at all. It was too high a price for her to ask of anyone.

She sat there, silent and quite oblivious to the hum of whispered voices around her as the first of the students walked forward to follow Ran's instructions.

What to do? She suddenly realised that he hadn't been being facetious when he had made that comment about knowing voices. At a distance, and given the improbable acoustics of the converted old house, he'd obviously not recognised her voice. Nor should he, considering he could hardly have expected to find a discarded lover among his new student group.

But to stand there, within reach of him, close enough to reach out and touch him, or be touched by him . . . that would be much more difficult. He couldn't fail to recognise her voice, at least enough to rouse his suspicions.

And why bother? Certainly she wouldn't now return to his classes. It would be ludicrous in the extreme, a form of self-torture beyond the bounds of sanity.

And yet if she did return, perhaps something he might say would reveal why he was here, why he had left the comfort of Sydney to venture into what he had once described as the wilderness of Queensland. Brisbane? She could see him going there, perhaps. But to a tiny provincial city another few hundred miles even further from his concept of civilisation? It made no logical sense.

'And neither does staying here,' squealed her survival voice. True! Better by far to flee, to get as far from Ran Logan as she could.

She looked up to see the redhead, tall, slender and quite elegant, step forward to recite her lines for Ran. The woman fairly oozed confidence, Rena thought, not unaware of her own shortcomings where that commodity was concerned. Surely this woman—Louise something—wouldn't get a tummy full of dancing butterflies every time she stepped on to a stage to sing. Presuming she could sing, of course.

Certainly, thought Rena, she could act. Every gesture, every movement was carefully choreographed to attract the maximum attention. Even with her voice, she seemed to be deliberately casting for attention. And those legs! Ran would have loved those legs, she thought.

And then: My God, what am I saying? I've been thinking about him as if he were dead and he's sitting right there in front of me. Not dead, but alive, completely, obviously alive. Or perhaps not quite completely. How can a man truly appreciate lovely legs that he can't see?

It was a sobering thought, coupled with the memory of his obvious appreciation of her own slender legs so very long ago. And once again she felt a stab of . . . no, not pity, but . . . almost resentment. It seemed . . . wrong, somehow, that a man with such an appreciation of the beautiful things in life should now be forced to bypass such pleasure.

Then she saw him smile, though she didn't hear the words that prompted it.

Typical, she thought, and choked back an audible snort of derision. Lord, even without his sight Randall Logan could charm the birds from the air, and this particular redheaded bird was all too obviously charmed. She was smiling down at him now with a look that would have a sighted man frothing at the mouth, champing at the bit. Really, Rena thought, the woman was being horribly obvious.

Ran must have thought so too. Cutting Louise off rather abruptly, he gestured imperiously for the next recitation. Rena felt a quiet little surge of pleasure at his reaction, then immediately replaced it with a silent growl of anger. How could he be so arrogant, so supremely confident in himself?

Or was he? Even a blind man couldn't have missed the invitation in the redhead's delivery. And certainly not a man like Ran, whom Dick had drunkenly accused on that first occasion of having to beat off the girls with a huge stick. He would be only too aware of Louise's invitation, yet he had deliberately forestalled it.

He was far more generous, Rena noticed, when the first of the older, presumably married women stepped up to speak into his recorder. Smiling, genuinely friendly, he did his very best to put the lady at ease, and seemed to succeed well enough.

But suddenly, all too soon, it was Rena's turn. And at first she simply sat there, dumbstruck and having to consciously will her trembling limbs to carry her forward.

Her eyes flew to Ran, and she was certain he'd snap out some appropriately sarcastic remark if she didn't move in a hurry. Surely he would! And just as surely, everyone must be watching her, wondering at her curious reticence. But no one was.

Why then did it seem to take her a year to walk those few steps to the front of the room? How, indeed, did she manage to walk at all? Her legs were like rubber; her heart thundered in her breast and her tongue was suddenly thick and lifeless, a dry, inarticulate mass that threatened to choke her.

But this is ludicrous, she thought suddenly. He can't see me. And even if he does think he recognises my

voice—so what? He can only *think* it; he can't possibly
be sure . . . ever. Which somehow made her feel a great
deal more comfortable about the whole exercise.

In fact, *let* him suspect. Let him wonder. She
wouldn't be coming back, and she would always have
that satisfaction, the knowledge that she had left him
with a niggling suspicion he could do nothing at all to
allay. And serve him right, too!

So why then did she recite her lines in a voice
deliberately pitched just halfway between her light,
normal speaking voice and the much deeper contralto
of her singing tones? She didn't even realise it until
she had done her thing and returned to her seat, and
when she did realise, she couldn't explain it even to
herself.

And he didn't even notice! That was the thought
which dominated her mind as she sat and watched the
remainder of the class speaking into the recorder. He
didn't even notice.

Rena had carefully watched his face throughout. And
not only his face, but his hands, his very physical poise.
But in no way at all had he revealed the slightest interest in her voice as opposed to those of the others.

Even the redhead got more reaction than that, she
thought, only to rebuke herself mentally for such a
childish reaction. Why on God's green earth should
she care anyway? Randall Logan was no longer a part
of her life. He'd made sure of that himself . . . very
sure indeed.

So he was blind now. So what? He hadn't been blind
when he'd swept her off her feet, spinning her into
bed with every possible ploy that a whirlwind romance
could provide, then simply disappeared without so
much as a farewell, thank you or wasn't it nice?

There would be some perfectly logical reason for his
presence here, here in the city where Rena had spent

her childhood in innocent happiness, and to which she had returned in search of that self-same innocence to help her ease the pain of her betrayal. Ran always had a perfectly good reason for his actions.

Always! He was the most self-assured, controlled man she had ever encountered. Strong, self-reliant, dominant—a man among men, always in control of himself and his life.

Certainly, she thought, he had controlled her. Right from the very beginning he had orchestrated his campaign to make her like him, then fall in love with him, then succumb to his physical advances. All planned . . . all controlled. Bastard!

He had never, quite literally, so much as touched her when he invited her out to dinner. He offered the invitation before driving her home that third night at the tavern, and of course she had accepted. They had been properly introduced, after all, though that was of little significance compared to the sort of togetherness they had somehow shared as she sang.

Rena considered herself a reasonably modern girl. She believed in good manners, a responsible attitude towards one's actions. But despite being a virgin she wasn't a prude. And until she had encountered Ran Logan she had always thought herself a fair judge of men, as well. You met all kinds in her jobs, both as a legal secretary and on her evenings in the tavern.

But she had never met one like Ran. He had come for her in a hired, chauffeur-driven car. Not quite a limousine, but very flashy, and he had merely laughed at her protestations about waste when he had casually ordered the driver to busy himself until eleven-thirty and then be punctual to collect them.

'I make too much money for my needs,' he chuckled. 'And what's the sense of working for it if I'm not to be allowed to use it for things I enjoy? One thing I don't enjoy is trying to divide my attention between a lovely companion and every drunken nong that drives in Sydney at night.'

He had arrived complete with flowers, a tiny, delicate corsage of tropical orchids. White, correctly neutral since of course he had had no idea what she would be wearing. And yet somehow personal as well. As if he had really thought about what Rena might like and remembered her saying she liked orchids.

Ran had been dressed to perfection—dark trousers, a splendidly-cut midnight blue tuxedo, shoes that gleamed almost with a life of their own. His only jewellery had been a silver ring with an unobtrusive chunk of boulder opal set in it. Not flashy, but certainly impressive on his slender, artistic finger.

Rena had chosen her best dress for the occasion, a clinging sheath in basic black jersey with a soft cowl neckline and almost but not-quite-butterfly sleeves. It wasn't terribly sexy, she'd always thought, but it did wonders for her own colouring and she had always felt superbly comfortable in it.

Even more so, when Ran caressed her with a casual journey of his eyes from crown to the toes of her evening sandals and voiced an approval that was neither effusive nor abrupt, but somehow . . . just right.

They had dined at one of the best, most exclusive of the city's clubs, a place where Ran might well enough be recognised, but where certainly he wouldn't be forced to deal with casual encounters from anyone.

Rena couldn't remember exactly what she had eaten that night; he had ordered for both of them in French too fluent for Rena to follow. But she could still, sometimes, remember the flavours, the textures and tastes—especially during the small, loneliest hours of sleepless nights, when she lay staring through the insect screens of her small flat, watching the tropical moon play in the waves of the ocean only a hundred yards away.

Strange, the tricks memory can play, she thought. She couldn't close her eyes and *see* the food, which had been expertly and most attractively presented. But the tastes had stayed, though now sometimes made bitter by the rest of her memories about Ran.

They had danced. Rena had always loved dancing, and since ballroom dancing was an activity encouraged during her youth, she had become good at it while still quite young; she had even competed as far from home as Brisbane once, when she was . . . twelve, thirteen?

And in Ran's arms that night she had danced as never before, as if she were ethereal, a plume of living smoke being carried in the currents of warm air off Sydney Harbour. He, too, had danced expertly. But of course, he did everything so well.

The music had been created for lovers. It was as if he had somehow arranged with the small orchestra to play exactly the right music for each moment of that memorable evening. Rena had wondered, once or twice since then, if indeed he had done just that. It wouldn't have surprised her.

They had danced closely, but not stiflingly so. Ran had no need to smother her in his arms to show her he thought she was attractive, desirable. The lightest of touches was enough for that; there was something like an electric current that flowed between them wherever they touched. She had felt it in her hands, in the soft tenderness of her waist where his fingers rested, in the softer softness of her thighs when his leg pressed there during the turns.

And it was in his eyes, in his breath against her ear, the touch of his cheek against her crown and the infinitely satisfying touch of her lips against the throbbing column of his throat.

They had danced and danced and danced, pausing only for the occasional sip of wine, and once when Ran stepped out briefly to readjust their schedule with the waiting driver. Into the small hours of the morning they had danced, hardly speaking, hardly needing to speak. They were together, and it seemed enough.

When he had taken her home, he had kissed her. Only the once, but very gently, yet thoroughly. And he had smiled his pleasure through eyes that to Rena had seemed to light the very sky, and lips that seemed to fit her own exactly.

And the next day he had sent her flowers, only now she couldn't remember what they were or even what they had smelled like. A false perfume, it must have been, like so many other things about him, in the end.

'Well, that'll give me something to work on during the week ahead.' He was speaking, now, the entire class finished reading into the mechanical ear of his recorder. How much better, Rena thought as she, too, returned to the present, if the machine could give him mechanical eyes as well.

'And since our time's almost up for this evening, I think we'd best start looking at something to keep you people busy as well. You're not going to learn much about writing by just sitting here listening to me,' he said.

'Now I've been told by the chap who gave this course last year that there isn't any sense in trying to get you people to do any . . . homework. Not on, he said, but I don't believe him. Some of you, of course, didn't really come here to see about improving your writing, and as I said earlier, some of you likely won't see the course through in any event. But some of you will!'

The pause then was solely for dramatic effect, and Rena, for one, knew it. Ran was a master of dramatics; he had that inestimable ability to reach out and touch an audience, even through the horribly impersonal medium of television, and hold people's attention.

He grinned now, and it was a mesmerising grin, a warm, enfolding smile that seemed to offer something to each of them, some personal gesture that would help to bind them to him.

Well, not me, she thought, only to lose the thought as he began to speak yet again.

'But then he was a man of little faith; a cynic like all journalists. I used to be that way, once . . .'

And now you're worse, I bet, thought Rena.

'. . . and now I'm worse,' he said, and she clapped her mouth shut in surprise, wondering if she'd spoken aloud and he was parroting her. But nobody else seemed to notice.

'However, I've learned that if anyone really wants to get somewhere, they'll take the fullest possible advantage of whatever help is available, and I'm committed to giving those of you with that attitude all the help I possibly can.'

And he would. Rena couldn't in honesty dispute that. She knew well enough that Ran had worked his way up the long ladder to success with little help from anyone, and he felt it his duty to try and provide others with what he himself had missed.

'So let's see . . . what first, I wonder,' he mused aloud. 'I don't want to scare anybody off too quickly, so we'll have to look for a small project that everybody can handle . . . I know! Something romantic. For next week I want everyone to write me something on a romantic theme.'

There was a silence as they absorbed his words, but it was Ran himself who broke that silence.

'It's an old saw that you should write about what you know,' he said with a grin. 'And unless memory serves me wrongly you're all of an age where romance

must have poked in at one time or other—rosy-hued
glasses and all.'

'Actually, I'd have thought I was a bit *too* old to be
writing about romantic things.' The comment was
from the tall, white-haired man in front of Rena, a
man she privately judged to be a fairly active sixty or
thereabouts.

Ran's laughter was a short, cynical bark. 'It should
be easier for you than any of us, John,' he countered.
'You've been alive longer and undoubtedly learned a
fair bit more as well. Or are you planning to tell me
that romance is dead?'

'Not a bit of it.' The reply was quick, in a voice that
bespoke a warm and generous nature. 'And you're
right, of course. I'll just have to kick my memory into
gear and see how it goes.'

'If you must,' Ran replied with a smile. 'But why
must you depend on your memory? Romance isn't only
for the very young. Even old fellows like you and me
can still have dreams and hopes.'

This time it was the older man who laughed, and
he had company from most of the other students.
'Too right!' he said, 'and thanks for reminding
me.'

Ran's own smile was somewhat less enthusiastic.
Almost . . . bitter, Rena thought. 'Don't thank me,' he
replied. 'Just write about it. I reckon all of you should
be able to manage five hundred words in a week.
Typed, double-spaced, wide margins all round. Say an
inch top and bottom, inch-and-a-half on the left side.
Nice and neat, since you're going to have to read it.
That'll give you two pages, but if you're going well,
don't stop, for God's sake. Do three, four, a dozen if
you're able.'

He reached out with agile fingers to shut the briefcase, then paused and appeared to be looking round

the room. Only he wasn't . . . not really, Rena thought.
He couldn't possibly be.

'That about wraps it up for tonight,' he said quietly.
'Unless any of you have questions? Please feel free if
you do have, because I've got all the time in the world
and I'd be more than happy to stay a bit later if necessary.'

'Well, I have one,' said the older man, John, 'although probably it's none of my business. But I
wouldn't mind knowing, just for curiosity's sake, what
somebody of your . . . status, I guess you'd say, is doing
here. I mean, after the bright lights of Sydney and an
international reputation and all . . . oh, hell, I guess I
didn't put that very well.'

Ran smiled. 'Oh, it was clear enough,' he said. 'Let's
just say that an international reputation doesn't always
demand international facilities. And now, at least, the
bright lights you mentioned aren't so very bright any
more.'

It wasn't a rebuke, although the older man hastened
to voice a partial apology that was carelessly waved
aside. 'No,' said Ran, 'there's nothing to apologise for.
I honestly just thought I needed a rest, a change of
climate. I once heard about your city from . . . someone,
and it seemed like a place worth visiting, that's all.'

'You're not here permanently, then?' This time the
redhead, Louise, her voice sultry and suggestive.

'I don't know yet,' Ran replied. 'It's possible . . .
anything's possible. Certainly I like what I've seen so
far. Perhaps I'll stay.'

Louise didn't continue the discussion, and indeed
looked ever so slightly put out.

Humph! She's probably shirty because he didn't
appear to remember her name, thought Rena. But he
remembered it all right. He's just not showing all his
cards at once.

And she felt a tiny twinge of pleasure at Ran's easy manipulation of the smarmy redhead's feelings. It was a feeling that disappeared seconds later when her own name came to Ran's sensuous lips, quite unexpectedly.

'Could I get somebody, perhaps you, Rena, to lock up the back door as you're leaving?' he asked. 'I'll catch the other one myself when I go. Oh, and perhaps you'd catch the lights as well, so that I don't inadvertently leave one burning to no good purpose?'

'All right,' she replied, blurting out the reply in keeping with the surprise she felt. He had remembered *her* name, but why choose this particular occasion to reveal the fact?

Ran sat immobile during the scuffling confusion as everyone collected their gear and started leaving the building, and Rena did as he'd asked about the back door and lights. It meant having to fumble her own way to the verandah door in stygian darkness, but that was nothing compared to the strange feeling she had over leaving Ran sitting silent in the black, empty house behind her.

She was still standing in the verandah doorway when the harsh scraping sound of a match being struck caught her ear, and she turned to watch as Ran expertly touched the flame to the end of his cigarette. Strange, she thought, he didn't once smoke during class. Perhaps it was because he couldn't always be certain of lighting his cigarettes without fumbling, she wondered, and had to stifle a brief surge of pity.

Pity, for a man like Randall Logan? Not likely. Not even if she didn't hate him so much for what he'd done, she thought. Pity was the last thing Ran could accept from anyone, regardless of the justification.

'Are you having problems, Rena?' The voice came from the blackness behind her, Rena having once again turned towards the door and the safety of the street.

'Umm . . . no,' she replied hastily, and then to her own surprise added, 'I was just wondering if you'll be all right. I mean, it seems rather . . . horrid to just go away and leave you sitting in the dark like this.'

The laugh that replied to her lame remark was harsh with bitterness. Harsh and somehow cruel, she thought.

'You forget, dear Rena, that you *always* leave me in the dark,' Ran's voice grated. 'And I assure you I'm getting quite used to it by now.'

'Yes, I suppose so,' she replied, 'but that doesn't make it any more pleasant.'

Again that grating, jeering laugh. 'Pleasant? No, I suppose not,' he replied. 'But on the other hand it's not that awful, either. Provided of course I don't have to go anywhere in a hurry. That gets a bit tricky.'

'You really sound horribly bitter,' said Rena, and could have kicked herself. What an insensitive remark! 'But then I suppose you've every right to be,' she added hastily.

Even in the darkness she could sense his shrug. 'One gets used to anything, in time,' he said. 'Might I suggest if we're to continue this conversation you come back in here and sit down? It's bad enough not being able to see you, without having to shout.'

Not on your life, she thought, but said, 'Of course,' and found her eyes had adapted enough to the darkness so that she could retrace her steps to the room without banging into anything.

She could even, she thought, see Ran smile grimly as she slid into the desk she had vacated only moments before.

'Tell me about yourself,' he said then—abruptly, almost curtly.

'I already have,' she replied, hoping her voice didn't

reveal the surge of caution his words provoked. 'Perhaps it's your turn now.'

He snorted. 'There's very little to tell. I'm blind;
I'm here. I've written a couple of books and before
that I was a journalist, of sorts.'

And I thought I was evasive! Rena thought.
Suddenly she could almost sense his withdrawal, the
turning inward to where something very obviously
hurt him a great deal. She spoke more quickly than
she had intended, and with less care, in hopes he would
stop the pulling away, the almost tangible closing up
of his emotions.

'How . . . how did you lose your sight?' she asked
abruptly.

This time his bark of laughter was undeniably bitter,
so laced with hurt she could almost taste it.

'Which time?' he demanded, causing her mouth to
drop open in astonishment. He had never mentioned
during their brief and ill-fated affair that he had ever
suffered such a thing. But could he have been blinded
. . . twice? . . . three times? . . . in the two short years
between?

'I . . . I don't quite know what you mean,' Rena
faltered.

His voice now grated; he almost spat out the words.
'I mean, quite obviously, that I've been blinded more
than once,' he snapped.

'Well, I'm sorry, but I didn't know that,' she retorted,
unable to hide the nervous anger. 'I'm sorry if the
question upset you; perhaps I'd better go after all.'

'Don't be hard to get along with.' Ran's voice was
normal now—or perhaps it was simply his use of a line
so very familiar to her. He had even used it, she
recalled, in bed, once.

But she didn't reply, and finally it was he who spoke,
this time without anger evident in his voice.

'No, it's I who should apologise. I'm afraid I'm getting a bit testy in my old age.' And he chuckled, almost friendly. 'Perhaps I should explain that I've been blinded twice, or more likely in two reactions to the same circumstance. The first time was . . . oh, quite some time ago in what I suppose could be called an accident. That only lasted a month and a bit and I thought I was fully recovered. But then something must have set it off again, and this time it appears to have become permanent.'

Rena hesitated before asking, but finally couldn't control her curiosity. 'That must have been horrible,' she said. 'But how long between the two incidents were you . . . all right?'

'About a month.' He replied promptly, but now seemingly with little interest in the discussion. Almost before the last word had left his lips he had replaced it with a cigarette and was reaching for his matches.

The first match broke without lighting; the second he couldn't fit to the end of his cigarette before the flame began to flicker at his fingertips.

Rena shifted in her chair, her heart reaching out to him. But common sense prevailed, and she sat in silence, watching, as he finally got things under control with the third match.

'I'm sorry,' he said then, quite unexpectedly, 'I should have asked if you wanted a cigarette. Do you?'

'Actually, yes, I wouldn't mind at all,' she found herself replying, and left the sanctuary of the desk to walk over to where Ran was sitting, the open cigarette pack in his outstretched hand.

Rena took out a cigarette, but when she reached for the matches, he already had one out and was deftly striking it. When he reached out to hold the match towards her, his hand was at exactly the right height; she had only to stoop slightly to reach it. It was as if

. . . as if he knew her exact height, she thought. But that, surely, was absurd?

Only while she was thinking, the flame was burning ever closer to his fingers, and without thinking she reached out to grasp his hand as she leaned forward to blow out the match.

Only for an instant, but it was too much for Rena. It was as if the flames had scorched her own hand when she touched him, and her soft exhalation was supercharged into a heavy, sighing blast before she snatched her hand away, trembling.

'Is something wrong?' His voice matched the cocked head, the expression of concern on his face.

'No . . . nothing really,' Rena blurted. 'It's . . . just that you almost burned your fingers.'

'Which ought to teach me to play with matches, I suppose,' he replied with a wry grin. It was so deliberately provocative that she couldn't help but laugh aloud, and an instant later they were both laughing . . . together.

But it only lasted a moment. Then Rena remembered who she was—who *he* was! Her laughter faltered, then died entirely in the painful memory of too many other shared laughters.

'I'm sorry,' she said. 'I suppose there's nothing really very funny about it, in reality.'

'That's only because you've never seen me go through an entire box of matches trying to get one cigarette going,' said Ran, but the look on his face at the memory was anything but humorous.

'Wouldn't it have been a great deal easier to simply use a lighter?' Rena asked, memory supplying a picture of the heavy, solid gold lighter he had used to carry always.

Ran didn't reply immediately, and when he did there was a stubborn tang to his voice. 'It would have been,' he agreed, which told Rena that was exactly why he had chosen the other, more difficult alternative. Even hampered by blindness, Ran Logan would scorn any easy approach that taught him nothing.

Typical, she thought, unable to hold back the little surge of pride she felt in him. The road to success seldom favours those who take the easy route, and Ran, to her certain knowledge, made it a point of principle never to shy at any real or imagined difficulty.

'How long have you lived here?' he asked then, and it was a question so unexpected that she flinched, eyes flaring in wariness. Then she relaxed.

'I was brought up here,' she replied, honestly enough, although she was hedging tremendously. What her answer implied, deliberately, was quite different from the fact that she had spent only her childhood in Queensland; her childhood and these last two years.

'How about you?' she asked quickly, hoping by her own query to forestall any other questions from Ran. 'Have you lived here very long?'

'Couple of weeks,' he replied casually. Too casually? Rena eyed him warily, suspicious now without any concrete reason to feel that way.

'It must be quite a change from Sydney. That's where the older chap said you were from, if I remember rightly,' she said.

'Among other places,' he shrugged. 'Yes, it is something of a change, although a pleasant one. At one time I'd have thought all places would be the same to a blind man, but with other senses to compensate you'd be surprised just how different they can be. This place is heaven compared to Sydney on the noise factor—or lack of it—alone.'

Rena chuckled. 'Yes, it's certainly a lot quieter,' she said, then hastily added, 'I imagine.'

'I take it from that you've never been to Sydney,' he

said, probing again, unable to resist the curiosity within him about everyone, everywhere.

'I've been to Brisbane,' Rena hedged. 'It's certainly a lot more noisy there than here.' Truth, but still hedging.

Ran didn't miss her evasiveness, either. She could see by the expression on his face that his ears were picking up the nuances of her faltering replies. Deliberately, she let her speech slip into the cadence of country Queensland. Not too far, but enough to confuse him at least.

'I suppose you're right for a ride home?' she asked, mouthing the words through barely-moving lips and chewing them slightly on the way out.

Ran didn't even seem to notice. 'My secretary will be picking me up shortly, I should think,' he replied without expression. 'I wasn't sure how long this first class would go, so I told her to leave it until ten-thirty or later.'

Her! Her? Rena couldn't help but wonder if the woman to whom he referred was the same secretary he had had back in Sydney. The woman she had never met, but whose voice she would never, ever forget. The woman with the voice of a true professional secretary-cum-protector; the woman who had so coldly, deliberately put her off each time she had tried to get through to Ran by telephone after he had failed to return as promised. The woman, she thought with sudden fury, who had literally laughed at Rena's pleas to speak with Ran, obviously looking on the caller as just one of his host of feminine admirers.

'Of course he'll be calling you, Miss Conley,' the woman had inevitably replied. 'Yes, I've given him your message, but no, he's left no reply with me. No, I can't disturb him just now. You'll just have to be patient, Miss Conley . . .'

In the depths of her confusion, Rena had at first taken the woman's calm, cool replies as being understanding and truly concerned, but as reality intruded upon her shattered, heartbroken life, she had finally realised that she was only being laughed at. That Ran wasn't coming back to her, had no intention of coming back. And that this remote, cold-voiced guardian of his time was only carrying out his express orders.

And laughing at her. That, Rena had decided after her final, devastating telephone call, was obvious. That woman hadn't cared for Rena's feelings any more than had Ran himself. He had got what he wanted from her, and probably even went so far as to tell his secretary so they could share a laugh over the silly, stupid, naïve country girl who had tossed away her virginity to the first suave line that was thrown her way.

Rena looked at her watch, squinting in the dim light and twisting her wrist to catch whatever illumination might be gained from the single street light on the road outside.

'It's nearly that time now,' she said. Then, more strongly, 'And certainly time I was away, so if you don't mind . . .'

'No, I'll be fine,' was the reply. 'Have a good week, Rena. I'll . . . see you next Wednesday, then. And don't forget your homework, eh?'

'I'll certainly try and remember it,' Rena replied, with no intention of doing any such thing. 'Goodnight, then.'

Without waiting for a reply, she stepped out into the verandah and gingerly made her way down the narrow steps to the ground below. How, she wondered, did Randall Logan manage to negotiate these treacherous steps? Or did he have help from his secretary? Perhaps that, more than anything else, was his reason for deliberately staying until everyone else had left, but somehow Rena didn't quite believe it. She simply couldn't imagine Ran allowing himself to become totally dependent upon anyone.

She started back towards the main college grounds where her car was parked, but she had only gone a few steps when some inborn mischief turned her round again and directed her steps to the pool of shadow beside the house, where overhanging shrubbery quite concealed her presence.

Thought about logically, such sneaking about in the night seemed totally ludicrous, but from this vantage point Rena knew she could see Ran's secretary when she arrived. Just what this might accomplish, Rena honestly didn't know; she would be none the wiser, having never met Ran's super-efficient Miss Dunn while in Sydney, unless he were to call her by name tonight.

Several times during the next few minutes she almost gave it up. Such silliness, this hide-and-seek in the darkness, she thought. But somehow she didn't, and was snug in her shadowy lookout when the dark, sleek Jaguar pulled up outside and an equally sleek, equally expensive-looking woman got out of it with a gesture of extreme impatience on her lovely face.

CHAPTER THREE

STYLE—that was the only word for it, Rena decided. Bags of style. The woman fairly oozed it, from the crown of her erect head to the expensive high-heeled shoes on which she was gingerly making her way to the verandah.

There was nothing secretarial about her clothes,

either. A long-sleeved, low-necked blouse glowed faintly pink in the street lights, and over it was a knee-length smock in pale turquoise with some floral pattern. The expensively casual effect was enhanced by soft evening trousers that draped to narrow cuffs around narrower, quite dainty ankles.

Auburn hair, Rena decided. Perhaps leaning a bit to the carrot shades and worn short to emphasise natural curliness. And if not quite beautiful, the woman was certainly stunning, with an exquisite bone structure and a figure any man would find provocative in the extreme.

She watched in unbreathing silence as the woman picked her way to the staircase and started up.

'Randall? Are you there?' That voice! It was no longer in doubt; this was the same Miss Dunn who had so expertly put Rena off after Ran's abandonment of her two long years before.

'Did you expect me to be somewhere else, Valerie?' Ran's voice held overtones of sarcasm that somehow surprised Rena. Sarcasm and ... bitterness? It certainly seemed so.

'Well, you must admit it would be difficult to tell. What in God's name are you doing sitting there in the dark?' There was a petulance in that voice, definitely, and some faintly disguised impatience as well, Rena thought.

And if she could pick it out, surely Ran couldn't miss it. Nor did he!

'It hardly matters very much,' came that all-too-familiar voice. 'Whether the lights are on or not, I'm *still* in the dark.'

'Which is no reason to inflict the same punishment on others,' snapped the woman. Suddenly light flared from inside the building, and Rena slid deeper into her covert.

'Lord love us! What an incredibly dingy little hole,' said the woman, disgust evident in every tone. 'Really, Randall, I think they're taking advantage of you. Bad enough you've agreed to teach these bumpkins, but to have to do it in such surroundings, well . . .'

'Oh, leave it, Valerie,' Ran replied wearily. 'And I'd suggest you watch your tongue when speaking of the locals. The world doesn't start and end within the boundaries of Sydney, in case you've forgotten. I imagine most of the people here are justly proud of their community, however small.'

'Well, I can't imagine why. Frankly I think you're lucky not to have to see it, Randall. Not that there's very much to see, in any event. I have just spent the most incredibly *boring* evening waiting for you to get this over with.'

'Bored? You?' Ran's voice held tones of sarcastic disbelief. 'What did you do, go back to the flat and sit down with a book or something?'

'Certainly not! I've been closeted in a pub with all sorts of weird people, listening to some rather good jazz.'

'What's boring about that? I'd have thought you'd be enjoying yourself; you've always loved jazz.'

'Oh, the music was quite good, at least for such a tiny, provincial little town. But the people! You simply wouldn't believe them, Randall. Most were dressed in the most outrageous clothing . . . not a tie amongst them. It was all terribly . . .'

'Casual, I presume,' he interjected. 'Which is hardly surprising. And from my own viewpoint, quite refreshing.'

'Yes . . . well, that's your viewpoint. I found it quite unimpressive. But enough of that. Come along and I'll guide you down these frightful stairs and out to the car.'

'The hell you will!' he snarled, and Rena found herself wide-eyed at the anger in his voice. 'Just get the lights and I'll guide *you* down the steps. I judged from the last person who tried them in the dark that they're a bit tricky.'

'They're downright dangerous,' snapped the woman. 'And frankly I think you should complain to the college authorities. I mean, what if you were to fall and injure yourself? And for what? Surely you're not expecting to find much budding talent among the people *here*?'

'You're a snob, Valerie.' He said it mildly, entirely without rancour. 'Sometimes I wonder why you came with me.'

'Why, to take care of you, of course,' was the unsurprising reply, couched—to Rena's ears—in layers of velvet over steel.

The two conversationalists were at the bottom of the steps now, so close Rena could almost have reached out and touched them. Valerie Dunn had her arm linked through Ran's in a manner that was more possessive than helpful, and Rena found herself thinking how obvious it all was.

Power! This woman, clearly, had Ran in her power. And more—she was enjoying it, really enjoying it. Rena felt sick. Even hating Ran as she did, it was somehow . . . indecent to think of him at the mercy of this . . . this creature.

She found herself watching in helpless rage as the woman handed Ran into the passenger seat of the Jaguar, then lithely stalked around the car to seat herself behind the wheel. Like some prowling jungle cat, Rena thought. Some predator with a helpless victim at its mercy.

Just before the door closed, she saw in the car's interior lights the woman's gloating expression, and something inside Rena went out to Ran, sympathy overriding pain and hatred.

She heard Ran asking if Valerie Dunn had been able to find out ... something! But the answer was lost in the purring acceleration as the car moved off.

Rena waited for several minutes before she, too, left the shadows to walk hastily along Walker Street to where her car now sat alone in the huge, empty college parking area.

There was little traffic on the long drive home, which was perhaps just as well, she thought, considering the trouble she had keeping her mind on her driving. But her elderly, almost matronly Holden station sedan—*Matilda*, she'd named it—seemed to know the route without Rena's guidance, and before she realised it the vehicle was turning into the driveway of Rena's home at The Oaks.

Her flat was the second storey of quite a large house on the esplanade near the Oaks beach, a man-made, narrow gut of sand gouged out from the rubble of black volcanic boulders that formed most of the coastline. The house itself belonged to a Sydney businessman who used the lower floor only during his annual winter holiday, and Rena's role as caretaker kept the rent barely within her budget.

On most evenings she would sit on the high verandah outside her lounge room and bedroom, luxuriating in the cool sea breezes and watching the occasional huge ship as it wended its way through Burnett Heads to the Bundaberg Port.

But tonight there were only the flashing lights of the river entrance, lights that seemed to mock her every attempt at lucid thought.

It just didn't seem possible for Ran to be teaching in Bundaberg. Much less blind! The very thought sent shivers through her.

And for her, of all people, to wander so unwittingly into his class! That was simply pushing coincidence too far.

And why Bundaberg, of all possible places? Could it be that he had somehow remembered her saying she had been born there, brought up there? It didn't seem likely; she certainly didn't remember ever mentioning it. Even if she had, why should he *now* choose to seek her out?

It was two long years since he had walked out of her life without a single word. Walked out—and stayed out, with plenty of assistance from his haughty secretary Valerie Dunn.

Suddenly the sea breeze took on an ominous chill, cooler than usual despite the mid-winter expectations of near-tropical Queensland. Rena shivered and went inside, closing the sliding aluminium windows against the worst of the breeze.

But she couldn't turn off her mind, even when she had got ready for bed and snuggled down beneath her eiderdown quilt. Ran Logan. The name swirled over and over, round and round in her mind like some evil chant, a litany of deceit and despair.

She wouldn't return to his class, of course. She told herself that during the long hours before sleep finally came, and repeated the statement next morning over her coffee and toast. And again that night and on Friday morning, and Friday night and Saturday morning.

But over the weekend she wrote a poem. Not for his class; that would have been senseless. It was, she decided, for her and her alone. One day, perhaps, she would put it to music, adding it to her repertoire. But Randall Logan would never hear it.

Her usual Monday night singing engagement at one of the pubs in town had gradually become a highlight

of Rena's lonely life since returning to Bundaberg—
but on this Monday evening it was sheer torture.

She found it impossible to concentrate; her eyes kept
straying towards the door, her heart leapt like that of a
startled wild animal with each new arrival.

It was ridiculous, she thought. How could Ran
Logan possibly turn up? Except by accident, of course.
Certainly it could only be by accident that he had
chosen to visit Bundaberg in his attempted escape from
the rigours of city living.

He simply couldn't have knowingly followed her.
Not after all this time. And he wouldn't have reason to
do so in the first place, not after the way he had so
casually broken off their Sydney affair.

In Rena's troubled state of mind, the evening passed
slowly and in a strange, melancholy, almost mystical
fashion. She couldn't—for the first time in her
memory—seem to reach her audience. Her songs were
haunting, all the old ballads, the sad songs and the
music of tortured souls. It was almost as if she sang
only to herself and for herself; there was no applause,
no indication that anyone was even listening.

It was so bad, indeed, that during the final break the
pub's manager came over to enquire if she was
deliberately trying to drive off his clientele.

'Personally, I quite like that type of music, Rena,'
he said sympathetically. 'But not as a businessman. It's
the wrong night for it and the wrong crowd. This lot
won't drink more because you make them feel sad; they
just go some place less depressing.'

'I'm sorry . . . really I am,' she replied. 'And it is my
fault; I just can't seem to get my act together.'

'That's obvious,' he grinned, 'so why not call it a
night and come have a quiet drink? If there's anything
I can do . . .?'

'No, I'm afraid there isn't,' Rena was forced to reply.

'It's just one of those nights, I'm afraid. I'll do better next week, for sure.'

'Of course you will. And if you can't come up more cheerful, maybe we'll get some rain for a change. People love sad songs in the rain, so long as it isn't a drought-breaker.'

She joined him and his wife for a drink, then pleaded a headache and left early. It wasn't a lie; she did have a raging headache. But it mysteriously disappeared as soon as she was no longer under pressure to try and maintain a mood she didn't feel.

Nonetheless, she slept badly, and found Tuesday's workload at the solicitors' office where she worked was almost too much for her weary intellect to cope with. It was all Ran's fault, damn his soul, she thought. Why had he come to Bundaberg? Why couldn't he simply have stayed out of her life?

She skipped dinner entirely on Tuesday night, a bad habit she had almost given up trying to break despite the certain knowledge that she was far too thin. Instead, she washed her mane of dark hair, gave serious if fleeting thought to having it cut next day, and without conscious thought found herself reworking her week-end poem.

By ten o'clock it was as perfect as she could make it and her eyes felt incredibly heavy, but something inside her forced her to bring out fresh paper and begin transforming the poem to prose, chopping and changing and muttering under her breath as she attempted to weave the essence of the poem into a short story.

Not for Ran's class, of course. She was determined there, even when she flounced muzzily from her bed next morning after only a few hours' sleep. Her resolve lasted until nearly eleven, when she had to walk through the city area to deliver some papers and almost crashed head-on into Ran Logan as she scurried out of one of the arcades.

She stopped, shocked by the closeness of the encounter but even more so by the fact that he seemed to
be looking straight into her eyes. The sensation was so
vivid that she spoke before realising it was only an illusion of his reflective glasses.

'Why, good morning, Mr Logan.'

Her words seemed to startle him, and Rena realised
that he had no idea at all how close he had come to
being physically run down by her hurrying figure.

'It's . . . Rena, isn't it?' he asked slowly, then reached
out as if to shake her hand. Without thinking, she
placed her fingers in his, half expecting something like
an electric shock and almost disappointed when she
encountered only human flesh.

'Yes,' she replied, then giggled. 'You weren't kid-
ding about being a quick study on voices, were you?'

His own laugh revealed white, even teeth. 'That
depends on whether you call eight hours a day for
seven days a quick study,' he replied. 'And I'll be more
honest if you'll promise to keep it to yourself; it was
the perfume as much as the voice.'

The perfume! Rena almost gasped aloud. Her mind
raced vainly as she tried to remember, then she
smothered a sigh of relief. Since returning to Queensland's subtropical climate and a much more casual life-
style, she had changed to a softer, more subdued perfume. He couldn't possibly make the connection that
way!

'Still, it's very impressive,' she said, half of her mind
demanding that she flee; the other half mesmerised,
wanting only to prolong the encounter.

'I don't suppose you've time for a coffee?' he asked
then, and the mesmerised section leapt into dictatorial
control.

'I think I could manage a quick one,' she found herself saying. 'The Elite Café is only just a few steps away.'

She made as if to take his arm, then immediately thought better of it and found herself standing in a somewhat confused silence. Should she guide him? Or would he be put off by any attempt at help? She didn't know what to do.

Ran solved the problem for her, reaching out his arm so as to link it with hers if she desired. 'I think you'd better aim me in the right direction, at least,' he said wryly. 'I still don't know the town quite well enough to have individual shops orientated. The pubs, yes, but then almost all of them are on corners and they all have a slightly individual sound to them as well.'

Rena didn't reply until they were inside the milk bar and seated at one of the small tables. 'You seem to be adapting marvellously well,' she said. 'I must admit, I wouldn't have expected to find you roaming about downtown on your own.'

Ran shrugged. 'I get by. Not much more than that, I sometimes think, but it's better than nothing.' He paused only slightly before changing the subject.

'Have you done your homework for tonight?' he asked as the waitress arrived with their coffee.

Rena hedged. 'Sort of,' she said. 'I'm working on two different approaches at the moment and I'm not entirely sure where I'll end up.'

Why she couldn't just come out and admit she wouldn't be returning to class, she didn't know herself, but something in Ran's attitude kept her from such disclosure.

'It doesn't matter which approach you wind up with, just so long as you finish one or the other,' he said. 'One of the biggest dangers for a writer starting off is to keep chopping and changing so much that nothing ever gets finished. Could I trouble you for the sugar, please?'

'Of course,' she replied—and almost asked if he'd like her to sugar his coffee for him. But no, let him work that out for himself, she thought, and was only mildly surprised to find that was exactly what he had had in mind.

He managed it quite skilfully, using his agile fingers to locate the sugar bowl in correct juxtaposition to his cup and then ladle in two spoons of sugar without spilling a grain.

'What made you decide to take on this course?' he asked abruptly, and Rena had to spend a moment marshalling her thoughts before she could find the right words.'

'I've . . . written a bit of poetry,' she replied. 'And I rather thought I'd like to try prose. Really it was just a spur-of-the-moment sort of decision. I saw the advertisement in last week's paper and made up my mind quite quickly. Not very exciting, I'm afraid. But what made you decide to teach it? I'd have thought . . .' She trailed off, unable to put in words her feelings that he would have more logically hidden behind his blindness instead of forcing himself to new challenges when he had enough already.

'I've always wanted to try teaching,' he replied. 'I knew the bloke who taught the course last semester and he mentioned it so I thought I'd give it a go.'

'I have the feeling it's going to mean a great deal of work for you,' said Rena. 'It must be difficult enough to cope with your own writing, much less that of a bunch of rank amateurs.'

He laughed, then, and it was something of the Ran Logan laugh that Rena remembered. Alive and vivid and wholehearted . . . vibrant with the sheer vitality of the man.

'Do you know the very best thing about being blind?' he asked, voice still throaty with laughter. He didn't wait for her to reply. 'It's that I seem to need so much less sleep. I've done more work in the past two years than I think I managed at any time before in my life, because I don't have the sun or the clock to tell me I should be tired.'

Rena shuddered. 'You make it sound almost ... pleasant,' she retorted, and her feelings must have been evident in her voice.

'Hardly pleasant; merely productive,' he grunted, and she was startled to see the pain on his face. Pain ... and bitterness. Randall Logan might be more productive, but it was obvious he didn't consider that much reward for the loss of his sight.

Suddenly he gulped down the remainder of his coffee and rose to his feet. 'I've taken enough of your time, I think,' he said. 'If you'd be kind enough to guide me out to the street again, I'll let you get back to work, as I must.'

Reaching into his pocket, he extracted sufficient notes to cover the coffees twice over, but obviously couldn't be bothered waiting for the change.

'Thank you for the coffee,' Rena said when they once again reached the footpath.

'And you for the company; I quite enjoyed it,' he replied with a grin. 'I'm sorry I got a bit short in there, but sometimes I find myself a victim of a sort of ... claustrophobia, I guess you'd call it. It's one aspect of this damned blindness I'm still having a great deal of trouble adjusting to.'

'It's all right,' said Rena—and then found herself quite at a loss for words to continue. Anything that left her mind seemed patronising by the time it reached her lips, so she stood in embarrassed silence until Ran finally made his farewell.

She stood and watched as he moved lithely down the footpath, using the white cane as if he had been blind all his life, then tears blurred her vision and she had to turn away.

All prior resolutions were swept aside when her lunch break came, and she drove back to the college to formally enrol for the creative writing course.

Only one single barrier loomed up during that exercise—the enrolment form that demanded her full name and address. Dared she write: *Catherine Conley Everett*? She debated the question so long that she looked up to find the clerk regarding her quite strangely.

Ran couldn't read it. She knew that. But if it were read *to him* . . . oh, no! Even blind, he couldn't fail to pick up the name Catherine Conley. Finally Rena decided; she simply put down *Rena Everett*. And to hell with the bureaucracy, she thought.

She had second thoughts about it all during the afternoon, and again when she slipped home after work for a quick, light meal, a change to more casual clothing, and both the poem and first-draft short story. Even further second thoughts filled her mind as she drove back in the early midwinter darkness and found herself the first to arrive for that evening's class.

She arrived even before Ran himself, and found herself huddling low in the seat of her station sedan when a glance in her rear-view mirror showed Ran's gleaming Jaguar, with Valerie Dunn at the wheel, quietly halt in front of the staff house.

How ludicrous it seemed! Valerie Dunn had never seen Rena, wouldn't know her from a bar of soap. Indeed, as the Jaguar spun away from the kerb after Ran's silent departure from the car, its driver never so much as glanced towards the elderly vehicle with Rena in it.

And now what to do? Rena sat alone in her vehicle,

unsure whether to make her way into the building where Ran Logan was alone, perhaps wondering if any of his students would return, or to sit and wait for somebody else to be the first inside.

The decision was made for her when another car swerved into position behind her own and the elegant redhead, whatever her name was, slid from behind the wheel. She, too, didn't bother to look Rena's way; instead she headed straight for the lighted doorway of the building, her arms full of folders and writing materials.

It was only too obvious that this woman . . . Louise, that was it, had deliberately arrived early in hopes of catching Ran alone. Rena could have kicked herself for the sudden twinge of indisputable jealousy that accompanied that thought.

'Well, she's welcome to him,' she muttered aloud, and for a fleeting instant was within a hair's breadth of doing what she knew she really *ought* to do—leave.

Then some inner demon took control, and an instant later she was out of the car and striding determinedly up the narrow stairs to the impromptu classroom, making just enough noise as she climbed the stairs that her arrival couldn't go unnoticed.

She entered the rear door to the two rooms that formed the classroom, and spoke a subdued 'Good evening' that clotted in her throat at the sight of the redhead lounging prettily on the edge of the table behind which Ran was seated.

One long, shapely leg was swinging casually as Louise leaned close to him, obviously interrupted in the process of reading something to him in an intimate voice. What it was, Rena couldn't have guessed; she hadn't heard more than a murmur since ascending the staircase.

The redhead shot her a vaguely hostile look, but it

was Ran's voice that broke the sudden silence. 'Good evening, Rena,' he said in tones that seemed distinctly welcoming. 'I'm certainly glad to have salvaged two students for the evening, or are both of you early and we've still something to look forward to?'

'I think we're both early,' Rena replied, not bothering to acknowledge the scowl that said, in Louise's eyes, only one of them was early and that was Rena herself.

Rena found herself wondering if he had greeted Louise by name with the same familiarity he had shown upon Rena's own arrival. Perhaps not, which might account for the unfriendly look the redhead was still giving her.

Before she could worry much about it, footsteps announced the arrival of yet another student, and within five minutes the full complement of ten had straggled in to take their places.

'Well, this is certainly encouraging,' said Ran when the count was made and he had been advised. Then he quickly set up his recording equipment and asked for a second chair to be placed beside his own at the large table.

'Now we come to the fun part,' he said with a grin. 'I know that some of you will be shy at first, but the best way to get over that is to get in first and get it over with. So who's first?'

It was too quick; too sudden. Looking round the class, Rena found every other student doing exactly the same, each one suddenly beset by the shyness Ran had mentioned.

Ran himself was also surveying the room, swinging his head around almost as if he could see. And his temper was quickly fading, Rena could tell, or was he simply as nervous about this experiment as his students?

Her first instinct was to sit silently and let him sweat it out, but even as that thought occurred to her, she knew she couldn't be so cruel to a man in Ran's condition, no matter what justification she might personally feel. A moment later she was on her feet, writing in hand, and moving up to seat herself beside him.

His whispered 'Thank you, Rena' was almost conspiratorial, but beneath it she felt an undercurrent of genuine thanks that gladdened her heart and dispelled whatever nervousness she felt.

After she had read her own compositions, the rest of the class were easily convinced to follow suit, and before half an hour had expired, the entire week's submissions were on tape.

'See ... didn't hurt a bit,' Ran commented. 'Now comes the part that will—the criticism. I want all of you to feel quite free to comment on the work of any other, or indeed your own—but let's keep it tidy and constructive. There's no gain in tearing somebody's cherished prose apart just for the sake of having something to say.'

And so it began. Ran let everyone have their say about Rena's writing before commenting himself, and when he did it was mostly to answer questions raised by other class members rather than comment on the work itself.

He did much the same with everyone else's work, using his knowledge to guide, rather than criticise, to explain rather than rip apart work that had obviously demanded a good deal of effort from most contributors.

Most of the writing, Rena was somewhat surprised to hear, seemed quite good. Not professional, certainly, or why would the would-be writers be attending Ran's class at all? But very definitely of a higher standard than she would have expected.

It seemed that Ran thought so, too. His general comments when all the submissions had been read were filled with praise for what had been done.

'It's a good start . . . an excellent start, as a matter of fact,' he said. 'If we can all keep up to the pace, you'll find you accomplish quite a good deal of writing during the eight weeks remaining of this course.'

All the submissions were piled together before him, and as he spoke, he lifted them and shuffled them through his long, slender fingers. Almost like a deck of cards, Rena thought, wondering idly why he had bothered to have the writings left with him in the first place.

She found out a few moments later, in a fashion that shocked her almost as much as it did the rest of the class.

'You'll all remember that on our first night I advised you—at least three times—to keep a carbon copy of everything you wrote,' said Ran, and there was a mischievous smile playing round his mouth as he said it.

Then the grin broadened, became positively devilish. Ran reached into his pocket and pulled forth a dollar note, which he brandished before him in a deceptively casual wave.

'I'll give three to one odds that at least one of you didn't keep a carbon of what I have here in front of me,' he said. 'And more likely two or three—perhaps even half of you. Any takers?'

He laughed at the gulf of silence that followed his question, then replaced the dollar in his pocket and once again picked up the typescripts from the table.

'I thought so. Which is certainly going to make next week's assignment a bit tricky for some of you.' And without a pause he ripped all the manuscripts to pieces and threw them down again.

Rena's gasp of astonishment was echoed from

around the room, then followed by a deep rumbling of anger from several throats. Most immediately vocal was the redheaded Louise, who was obviously among those who had ignored the advice.

'I think that was a filthy, rotten trick!' she cried, rising to her feet as if she intended to rush forward and rescue the shreds of her manuscript. Around her, several others fidgeted in their seats, and the hum of angry mutterings grew louder.

Ran merely grinned at them, outwardly as calm as old John, who had obviously kept a copy of *his* work and was now regarding the antics of his classmates with growing amusement.

'A dirty trick? Really, would I play a dirty trick on my favourite students?' he asked scathingly. He seemed quite oblivious to the aura of hostility that surrounded him.

'Now for next week, I want you to revise your work,' he said as if nothing untoward had happened at all. 'Those who have stories to finish should pay attention to what's been said today, and those who handed in finished work tonight should rework those same stories, again taking heed of the criticisms.'

'And how the hell are we supposed to do that when you've destroyed the originals?' Louise demanded petulantly. Her green eyes were blazing with fury and Ran didn't need his eyesight to recognise her anger.

'Well, I guess those of you who didn't listen last week will have to pray for good memories,' he retorted with scorn. 'I'll guarantee this much—you'll damned well remember to keep a carbon from now on.'

Rena shuddered at the atmosphere of anger that pervaded the room. It seemed so . . . so illogical, somehow. Why build up all their egos and enthusiasm only to tear it all down again by such a blatantly provocative gesture?

Yet she herself didn't share the anger so evident on half the faces in the class, despite the fact that she was one of the offenders. The thought of rewriting her poetry didn't upset her at all, and as for the short story . . . it could surely stand to be reworked in any event.

'Well, I still don't think it's fair,' declared Louise.

'Of course it isn't,' replied Ran, his face grim. 'But it's a lesson that obviously some of you had to learn, and better to learn it this way than by losing an entire book, or something you've written that's really important. Face facts! Things *do* get lost. The post office loses manuscripts; publishers lose manuscripts; editors lose manuscripts. Hell, I've even lost some of my *own* manuscripts—and that was when I could see.'

He paused, rubbing wearily at his forehead as if his fingers could so easily remove the lines of stress there. And when he spoke again, his voice was softer, less abrasive. 'Be honest with yourselves; with one possible exception not one of you turned in anything here tonight that wouldn't have needed rewriting anyway. This way you've learned a valuable lesson in the bargain.'

'And I suppose you're not going to tell us who the exception is, either,' snapped the redhead.

'I wouldn't have thought I had to,' Ran replied just as snappily. 'You all heard the submissions as well as I did.'

Rena found herself involuntarily glancing over to where John sat; certainly his partially-completed short story had been the only submission that *she* thought might merit such praise. But he merely returned her glance, his pale blue eyes twinkling still with amusement at the encounter between Ran and Louise.

Then, incredibly, it seemed as if the entire class was looking at her, though it was Louise who spoke, vitriolically.

'And of *course* you kept a carbon of your poem,' the redhead crooned, her voice fairly dripping with venom.

Rena looked round, disbelief surging through her. Surely they couldn't think . . . oh, no! she thought. She had to stifle the urge to giggle, so certain was she that the work Ran had mentioned must be John's story.

'Aren't you going to answer her, Rena?' Ran's rich voice held sarcastic overtones, but it wasn't that which sent shivers down Rena's spine. It was the barely-concealed sensuality of it, the hard-soft, living essence of masculinity which seemed to melt her bones even at that distance.

'No . . . n . . . o. No, I didn't,' she stammered. It couldn't be! Surely he was merely making some obscure point to Louise.

'And of course there's no question from anyone that it's Rena's poem I was referring to?' His voice sifted through the room, seeming to prick each student individually. To Rena's astonishment, there wasn't a single dissenting voice.

'And tell us please, Rena, why you didn't keep a carbon,' Ran continued, his voice like silk-smooth steel. 'And also, perhaps, why you haven't been screaming bloody blue murder at my destruction of your work.'

'I . . . I just never thought of it,' she replied. 'I've . . . never bothered in the past. And for the rest—well, I can always rewrite it; it wasn't all that good, certainly.'

'Therein lies that rarest of creatures, an honest woman,' Ran barked. 'If I hadn't been able to hear it with my own ears I don't think I would have believed it.'

Then his voice softened, became almost caressing.

'And do you think you'll remember to keep a carbon from now on?' he asked, and despite the reflective glasses and the knowledge of his blindness, she felt his eyes upon her.

'Well, I shall obviously have to if you're going to make a habit of tearing things up,' she snapped, temper frayed and touchy at having been made the centre of attention. Her sharpness brought a chuckle from old John and murmurs of approval from several others in the class, but Ran didn't so much as smile.

'I would hope that I never get into the habit of de-stroying beautiful things,' he said quite soberly. 'But for the benefit of the rest of you, I might also point out that I'd bet any amount of money Rena could re-write that poem entirely from memory without the slightest difficulty; I very much doubt if most of you will find it that easy with your submissions.'

'Well then, why should it be so easy for her?' Louise, the ever-angry redhead again.

'Because, dear Louise, Rena has already rewritten that poem, I'd guess, at least a dozen times,' replied Ran. 'Either that or she's far too brilliant to be here in the first place.' Then he smiled, and it was like a ray of sunshine in the room. 'Maybe both, for all I know,' he said. 'Certainly I'd have to think her reasons for being here involve marketing more than writing itself, assuming she's been entirely truthful in saying she's never sold any of her poetry.'

CHAPTER FOUR

HE knew! Rena shrunk into her seat, unable to force herself to look up and face his blank, accusing stare.

He knew! He must know, she thought, to have made a comment like that—so close to the mark. She closed her eyes briefly, certain that not only was Ran accusing her, but that everyone else must also be aware.

'Mind you, perhaps I malign the poor girl; I probably do,' he said then, and Rena's eyes flashed open in bewildered wonder.

Ran was rubbing at his forehead, where deep creases revealed a tremendous strain. Headache? Rena sucked in a deep breath at his frown of pain. But when he spoke, his voice was steady enough.

'In fact, I'm sure I do,' he said, surprisingly. 'It's just that I once knew a girl who made part of her living from poetry that was somewhat similar to that. Not quite as good, I fancy, but somewhat similar.' He shook his head, a lock of dark hair falling unnoticed down across his brow.

'Sorry, Rena. I think I . . . sort of let my mind wander a bit there,' he said. And again he shook his head, almost as if there was something annoying him, nagging at him.

'Anyway, that's enough for tonight if you all don't mind,' he said. 'You've got your work cut out for the week ahead, and I'm looking forward to seeing what next Wednesday brings.'

Louise's angry, long-legged stride set the pace for the rest of the departing class, although Rena was pleased to see that virtually everyone paused long enough to bid Ran goodnight.

She herself hung back, watching him. He *was* in pain, she suddenly realised, and without another thought she stepped hurriedly towards him.

'Are you all right?' The concern in her voice must have been obvious, but Ran seemingly chose to ignore it.

'Of course I'm all right,' he replied almost angrily. 'Except for the fact that I can't see, and there doesn't seem to be much we can do about that.'

'You're lying and you know it,' she replied with anger in her own voice. 'You may be blind, but I'm certainly not, and you've either been in very great pain or you do a marvellous imitation of it for a man who can't see.'

'Don't shout. I may be blind but I'm not deaf,' he countered. 'All I've got is a bit of a headache; I've had worse and it'll pass.'

'I think I've got some tablets in my bag,' said Rena. But even before she could get the handbag open he was waving off her intended gesture.

'Forget it! Pills don't help at all,' he growled. And then, with truly vicious bitterness, 'It's just my eyes trying to get control of themselves again—or that's what the quacks keep telling me, anyway. As if *they* knew anything about it!'

'I'm afraid I don't understand,' Rena said. 'Not that it's any of my business, of course, but . . .'

'According to the bloody doctors I'm not blind at all—except in my head,' he snapped. 'It's called psychosomatic blindness. I'm not blind; I'm crazy.'

Rena gasped. She couldn't help it. Indeed, she could hardly believe her ears. Randall Logan—perhaps the strongest, most self-assured person she'd ever met—and here he was saying his blindness was purely psychosomatic? That he was crazy?

'Oh,' she whispered. 'Oh, I'm sorry ... I ... I didn't realise.'

'There's nothing to be damned well sorry about; it's nothing to do with you,' he snapped, surly now, like a hurt animal wanting only to be left alone. 'And for God's sake don't go getting all clucky, or broody, or whatever it is women get when they're confronted with something like this; it doesn't help and it annoys hell out of me.'

'I have no intention of being clucky ... *or* broody.' Rena replied almost as hotly. Her own anger, she realised, was purely defensive, solely to keep her from revealing her true feelings. 'From the sound of things, you're getting quite enough sympathy from yourself, without me adding any.'

'Sympathy? Hah!' His snort of derision was a gesture both haughty and defiant. 'This isn't sympathy, dear Rena, it's plain, ordinary, old-fashioned anger.'

'And remarkably ineffectual as well, if you don't mind me saying so,' she replied. 'Being angry with the doctors isn't going to help you very much. I'm sure they're doing all they ...'

'I am not angry with the doctors,' he interrupted, his voice icy cold, grave cold. 'I am angry with myself. Because much as I detest the thought, I rather think the doctors might be right. And if it *is* all in my head, then I ought to be able to *do* something about it. Only I can't, it seems.'

Once again he reached up to brush a hand across his forehead, almost as if he were trying to clear away cobwebs from before his eyes. Rena shivered at the implications.

'Perhaps you've been trying too hard,' she said gently—and had to forcibly resist the urge to take him in her arms and add her own strength, her own will, to his.

Ran sighed. 'You might very well be right,' he said, his voice now softer, no longer abrasive and harsh with the inner devils that tormented him. 'And I apologise for taking out my bad temper on you.'

Rena smiled. 'That's all right,' she said. 'I've got broad shoulders.'

'Funny, I wouldn't have thought they'd be all that broad at all,' he replied in a voice she knew only too well. And before she could so much as think about it, he had reached out to take her shoulders in his hands.

His touch was gentle, but electric. Rena stood shock-still, feeling that she would melt at the sensations that flowed through her body. Her knees trembled, threatening to dissolve beneath her. She felt her nipples go firm against the light fabric of her bra, and something like a white-hot coal flowed down to steam in her tummy before lighting even hotter fires below it.

Then sanity drove like an arrow into her brain and with a sharp cry she flinched away from him, huddling crouched like a wounded, frightened animal.

'My God!' The words came loudly from his lips, and the expression on his face was one of amazement, incredulity. 'Rena, I'm truly sorry,' he said. 'I . . . I certainly didn't mean to frighten you.'

'It's . . . all right,' she gasped, unsure of her voice but knowing she must stop him from reaching out to her again. 'It's just that you startled me, that's all. Please don't worry about it.' And even as she spoke she was backing away, tiny, hesitant step by tiny, hesitant step. 'Please,' she said again. 'It's nothing to do with you.'

The lie followed her even as his voice did. 'I find that rather difficult to believe, under the circumstances,' he said. 'But either way I apologise.' And there was a coldness there, a slender thread of rejection recognised and felt.

Rena stopped, took a deep, slow breath, forced herself to return, to reach out and take his fingers in her own. 'But you must believe it,' she said softly. 'Because it's true.'

'Liar,' he said with equal softness, and his fingers pressed gently upon her own.

'Liar!' screamed a voice inside her, making no allowance for circumstances, no allowance for his feelings, for hers. She would have snatched her hand away, but he released it before she could.

'That's hardly very complimentary,' she said.

'The truth seldom is,' he replied, 'but I thank you for your good intentions, anyway. You're a remarkably empathetic woman.'

'I would have thought most women were reasonably so,' she replied, wondering at the same time why she was here, why she was carrying on this inane conversation with a man so completely, so utterly dangerous to her psychic well-being.

'Most women,' he said with astounding bitterness, 'are about as empathetic as starving lions, except when it serves their purpose.'

'Well, I'd suppose you'd know,' she found herself replying—and could have bitten her tongue.

Ran grinned, but it was a mocking, derisive grin. 'And that is a rather provocative statement,' he replied. 'Just what makes you think something like that?'

Rena stepped back, moving involuntarily closer to the doorway, to escape. Then some inner demon stepped into her mouth and took over her tongue.

'If you could see the effect you've been having on Louise, you wouldn't have to ask,' said her mouth. And her heart cried.

Ran's snort has genuine. 'Anything in long trousers would have that effect on Louise,' he retorted. 'She's about as subtle as a meat-axe.'

'Doesn't alter the fact she fancies you,' remarked Rena's demon-controlled tongue. 'Although perhaps a bit less since you tore up her manuscript.'

He laughed. 'More like a great deal less, but I dare-say she'll get over it. Any bets on whether she'll be back next week?'

'Not a chance,' Rena replied, now finding herself rather enjoying the game. 'She'll be back; no question of it.'

'And will you?' The question was unexpected, as was the softness of his voice, the intimacy of it. Rena had to pause for thought before replying.

'I expect so.' Just right, she thought. Noncommittal, emotionless.

'Good. I'd be rather upset if you didn't.' His voice was velvet, music. And her heart sang with the remark although she gave no visible sign of it.

'Yes ... well ... I suppose I'd best be going,' she faltered. 'Shall I ... do you want me to get the lights for you?'

'No, it'd just upset my chauffeur,' he replied. 'She seems to forget that being left in the dark doesn't bother me. Goodnight, Rena. I'll look forward to hearing what you come up with for next week.'

He might very well have meant it, too, she thought on the way home. But by dinner time the following Wednesday, she was in no way convinced he would be pleased with her work.

It had been, quite simply, a horrible, useless week. Rena's writing, actually, had suffered far less than her emotional situation, which by that third class of creative writing was walking a narrow tightrope and not doing it awfully well.

She had tried—every single evening, she had tried—to rework her short story along the lines suggested during the previous class. But every attempt she made seemed only to make the story worse, until by class time she was almost ready to give it away entirely.

The problem, in a word, was Ran. He had been in her thoughts constantly throughout the week, pervading her waking moments, invading her sleep. But worst was the memories.

It seemed as if by touching her the week before, by simply taking her slender shoulders in his hands, he had shattered every barrier her mind and body had raised against him. She had driven home with his voice in her ears, his face in her mind, almost with his very presence in the car beside her.

Later that night, and indeed on each night when she went lonely to her bed, she seemed to relive that amazing, glorious, almost unbelievable fortnight two years before. The fortnight in which Ran Logan had met Catherine Conley, wooed her, won her—and deserted her as callously as changing a shirt.

Even in retrospect, even with the addition of two years of introspection and bitter wisdom, Rena had trouble believing how false that fortnight really was. It just didn't seem possible that so much promise, so much happiness, could have been forged in deceit.

At the time, and even in her most secret memories, it had seemed so perfect, so totally . . . right. Ran had seen her daily after that first dinner date. He had sent her flowers, he had bought her presents, he had taken her to eat and drink and be entertained in a fashion that was at first quite overwhelming.

And yet it seemed that at the same time he had realised her need for occasional privacy, her need to maintain her own individuality, her own sense of person.

His presents had always been thoughtful, considered. Most, indeed, hadn't even been expensive, but mere trifles that seemed mostly to reveal that he listened to her, was aware of her needs.

During one of their evening strolls she had stopped to demand that he buy her some hot buttered popcorn, and he had laughed with her as they shared it, smearing butter everywhere and emerging from the experience like grubby little children. But two days later she had received an enormous five-gallon container of the stuff, specially delivered by messenger early one Saturday morning.

Included with the popcorn was a beautiful slinky silk scarf and a note advising her to use the scarf only for 'after-popcorn' grooming. When Ran had arrived an hour later she had still been uncertain what to do with such a ridiculous, illogical, loving gift.

He had shown her—hoisting the container on one broad shoulder as they strolled hand-in-hand to the nearest park, where they shared it with every passing child until the last kernel was gone.

Rena still had the container; it was in her bathroom collecting dirty tissues and discarded tights. Appropriate, she thought.

He had taken her sailing in Sydney Harbour, kissed her beneath the harbour bridge as the sea wind sent their small craft spanking across the water. He had taken her to walk in an isolated section of the Royal National Park during one long, sun-soaked, silent afternoon when they revelled in each other's presence and kept their attention consciously on the vivid natural world about them.

On the nights when she had to work, he had been there from beginning to end, encouraging her with his eyes, his every gesture revealing pride in her accomplishments, joy in her own pleasures of song and music.

They had seemed to share so much. Seemed to . . .

And yet the reality, in hindsight, was so terribly, cruelly and still unbelievably different.

He hadn't—for God's sake—even come to know her real name!

A small thing in itself, and one that Rena found herself now truly thankful for, but even in retrospect it seemed amazing that she could meet, love and give herself to a man without ever telling him that the name under which she sang was only a part of her name.

Catherine Conley had seemed an appropriate stage name. And when she met Ran Logan, she *was* Catherine Conley. But because he never once telephoned her at her day-to-day job, and no sane woman in Sydney would advertise her feminine status with a Mrs, Miss or Ms on her mailbox ... still, it seemed ridiculous. Rena's mailbox had borne the simple lettering *C. C. Everett*, since she never received mail as Catherine Conley.

But she never received mail from Ran, either. Nor was he ever present when she collected her mail. So she had never told him, not for any reason; and now it seemed ludicrous, although beneficial to the deceptive role she was in.

But it didn't help her writing any more than did her growing obsession with Ran, his blindness, and the curious circumstances that now threw them together on one single night each week.

Tonight! Tonight, and she had accomplished nothing with her short story but an enormous confusion of words and phrases and thoughts. Worse than when she had started.

Not, she supposed, that it mattered a great deal anyway. Certainly she must abandon any delusion that she was attending the classes because of her original intention to learn creative writing. No! The sole, simple attraction was Ran Logan, and Rena felt herself drawn like a moth to the flame.

As she drove towards the college for her third class, she felt bone-weary, exhausted by a week of near-sleepless nights, of days in which her mind flickered like a defective neon sign, unable to concentrate properly, to think properly.

And all because of Ran Logan! Truly, she thought, it was the blind leading the blind. The difficult part was that she, unlike Ran, should have been able to control her own mental blindness.

As usual, she was first to arrive at the college, although this time it was only seconds before the swooping black Jaguar veered to the kerb to deposit Ran. As before, she waited until he had fumbled his way up the steep, narrow staircase before leaving her own car and walking into the building to join him.

'Hello, Rena. You're early too, I see.' His welcome stopped her in confusion. How could he know? She had said not a word, hadn't, surely, approached close enough to give him the excuse of smelling her perfume. How?

He frowned slightly at her question, which she suddenly realised must have seemed a bit harsh without including an acknowledgment to his greeting. But when he replied there was no sign that he had noticed her abruptness.

He grinned, that slow, soft, gentle grin she remembered all too well, too painfully. 'I must admit that I wonder about that myself,' he said then. 'I wish I could explain it—as much for my own peace of mind as yours—but I honestly can't. It's just that there's something . . . familiar. I seem able to know when it's you, where you are when you're in the same room, things like that.' Then he laughed. 'Maybe I'm developing extra-sensory perception to make up for being blind!'

Rena laughed with him at that, but her own laugh

was taut and brittle. The very thought was frightening, almost terrifying.

And worse—far worse—with his next words.

'There's something about your voice, too. Something very familiar there.'

She shuddered, thankful he couldn't see her physical reaction.

'. . . perhaps because I once knew somebody with a similar voice,' he was saying. And then, without warning, 'Are you deceitful, like all women, Rena?'

She tried to pass it off lightly. 'No worse than most, I suppose. Not forgetting that I can't quite agree with you on such a broad generalisation in the first place. I don't happen to believe that *all* women, as you put it, are automatically deceitful.'

'Are you pretty?' The question came as if he hadn't even heard her reply. Or had blithely ignored it.

Rena didn't—couldn't—answer that one easily. Her mouth, suddenly dry and clogged with unexpected emotion, wouldn't allow it.

'I . . . suppose reasonably so,' she finally managed to say. 'I'm not unhappy with the way I look, at any rate.' Not quite the truth, especially after the week she'd just had, but not quite a lie, either. She knew herself to be anything but vain.

Ran *looked* at her; she could actually feel him trying to use his eyes, concentrating solely on his no-longer-existent sense of sight. His dark eyebrows furrowed and narrow lines of strain appeared beside his generous mouth.

'I'd have bet you were beautiful,' he said. Softly, very softly. A caress, almost, something inside Rena tried to reach out, to thrust itself from the scar tissue of his deceit and somehow touch him. She choked it back into submission.

'You know what they say about the eye of the be-

holder,' she replied, hastily, knowingly cruel, hurtful
and sorry and yet not sorry at all. Even blind he
shouldn't have this frightening ability to manipulate her
emotions.

Her words struck him forcefully. She could see the
sudden twitching of his strong jaw muscles, the con-
vulsive surge of the muscles at his throat as he choked
back a bitter reply.

'Yes,' he said finally in a voice like death. 'Yes, I
know what they say.'

And he turned away from her, striking the edge of
his table in his haste and then kicking out at it in silent
anger as he fumbled to find his seat.

Rena stood there in stunned silence, one hand raised
to her still-open mouth as if by the gesture alone she
could push the words back into it. Her mind was
stunned; vacated of rational thought by the unthinking
cruelty that had spewed from within her.

How could she *ever* have said such a thing? It was
. . . just not possible, she thought. And yet she'd done
it, and worse, done it coldly and without so much as a
thought for the pain it might inflict.

Bad enough to have perhaps rationalised it—fool-
ishly—as a means of alleviating her own pain, her own
wounds. But to use such a horrible weapon on a man
defenceless and blind . . .

'I . . . I . . .' She tried to get the words out, to apologise, even knowing there was little likelihood of it being
accepted. But too late. The sound of approaching footsteps heralded the arrival of other class members; Ran
ignored her without seeming to in his greeting of her
fellow students.

And he ignored her throughout the rest of the class,
merely passing off her short-story problems as 'expectable' and advising her that she was probably trying too
hard.

'You've chosen a sensitive subject, obviously one that you've some experience with,' he said. 'But you're too close to it, too emotionally involved. I realise that you're trying to use your writing to get things into perspective, but it must be too soon . . . for you.'

Then came the cruncher, the single, vengeful comment she had been waiting for all evening, a statement with a message that only Rena completely understood.

'It's obvious you've got a phenomenal—however justified—dislike of men,' he said. 'I'd suggest you keep on working at exorcising your bitterness for a while longer; maybe then you'll be able to get your perspectives organised.'

He didn't even really look in her direction as he spoke; he didn't need to. Rena got his message, and had to bite back a vitriolic retort.

It was no consolation that he was equally hard on several other members of the class. In fact only John and, surprisingly, the redheaded Louise had been spared his acid tongue. Rena wasn't surprised at all about John, who had obviously worked long and hard at his revamping, but Louise's work she recognised as being almost word for word what it had been originally, so close that Rena couldn't help wondering if the glamorous redhead had lied about not keeping a carbon.

But if Ran noticed the similarity he didn't comment on it, and the absence of obvious criticism had a distinct effect on Louise's personality. All of her abrasiveness seemed to vanish like smoke. She was smiling, pleasant, and—for her—only a little condescending towards the other members of the class.

What couldn't go unnoticed also was the diminishing size of the class. From ten down to only six, and the missing four seemed unlikely, in Rena's view, to return.

The unisex duo was gone, not surprisingly, but also missing were the nondescript young man with the motorcycle helmet, and one of the housewives. And judging from reactions to Ran's harsh criticisms this third Wednesday, she thought it likely there'd be another two missing by the next class.

One of the remaining housewives had taken on a sulky expression when Ran had contemptuously dismissed her excuses for not doing very much work, and the serious young student type also was looking none too pleased.

Certainly, Rena thought to herself, Ran Logan would be difficult to compare to the typical teacher in any institution. Her own memory included none with such vividness, such a blatant, careless regard for convention.

He was, this particular evening, dressed entirely in black. His slim, tight-fitting trousers fell on to shining half-boots, and a broad belt cinched them around the waist of a thick, fluffy sweater-shirt with a wide collar and deep-cut throat. Only the shine of the chain round his throat, the chain holding that *damned* medallion, and the silvery rim of his sunglasses broke the solid darkness of his figure.

Truly, she thought, he looked like the devil himself when strong emotion carved lines into his face and added even stronger lines to an already powerful jawline.

Even blind, he moved with the easy grace of a lean, hungry cat, having made a remarkable adjustment to the layout of the room around him.

What was equally obvious, although perhaps only to her, Rena thought, was that Ran was angry. More than angry, he was seething with a bitterness that—to her—was like a close-banked furnace, liable at any moment to blaze into uncontrolled fury.

And it was her fault: she hadn't needed his fiery personal remarks to tell her that. But what to do about it? Any attempt at apology now, she reckoned, would be met with only anger and contempt.

Still, she had to try for her own peace of mind. So when the lesson was over, surprisingly without any specific assignments for the coming week, she once again hung back to speak with Ran after the others had left.

It wasn't an easy thing to do. Especially since he seemed to know she was there, almost to have expected her to be.

'What's the story, Rena?' he demanded once the sound of footsteps had disappeared and it seemed they were alone. 'Did you stay behind to rub a little salt in the wounds, or just to complain about my assessment of your work?'

'Neither, and you very well know that,' she retorted, anger blazing up as she unconsciously covered her nervousness with defensive tactics. 'I wanted to apologise.'

'For what—the truth?' His voice was ragged with emotion, his entire bearing taut and tense. 'Don't bother, I've been handed worse lines in my time.'

'I really don't think that's the point,' she replied. 'What I said was . . . inexcusable.'

He grinned, not friendly, but savage, like some wild animal faced with its next meal. 'If it's the way you usually react to compliments, I'm surprised you've ever been close enough to a man to have built up such a storehouse of hatred,' he said.

Words leapt to Rena's lips—hot, angry, bitter words—but she choked them back. What, indeed, could she say? You shouldn't be surprised? If I'm really a man-hater it's your fault? I only hate one man, and it's you?

No, she would say nothing. That decision was made just as Ran decided it was the wrong decision.

'What? Nothing to say?' he demanded. 'Don't tell me all this bitterness is stored up inside a twenty-two-year-old virgin.'

That was too much! Rena's temper flung aside her good intentions, her common sense. 'Damn you!' she snapped, stalking towards him like an angry cat, one hand raised to claw out at his face. Only at the last instant did she turn her wrist so that it was the flat of her palm which struck him instead of her nails.

Ran stood like a statue as the sound of the slap rang through the emptiness around them. Only his reflective, mirrored glasses seemed to move, shimmering and rippling with the deepness of his breath. To Rena, it was like looking into deep, bottomless pools that distorted her own reflection.

The mark of her palm stood out like a brand on a face pale and taut with emotion. When he finally spoke, his voice trembled, but it was with restrained fury, not fear.

'That really took a lot of courage,' he sneered. 'Perhaps I should turn the other cheek.'

They stood there, each silent but panting with their anger, and Rena felt as if she might drown in those horrid, mirroring glasses.

It was Ran who broke the silence. 'Perhaps I've misjudged you,' he said softly. 'Maybe you're not quite as innocent as I thought.'

She had no chance to reply. His hands snaked out to take her by the upper arms, drawing her against him as his mouth searched unerringly for her lips.

Cruelly he forced her lips apart, ravishing her mouth and holding her so tightly she could hardly breathe. There was no warmth in his kiss, only a cold, soul-chill-ing passion, a barbaric sensuality that neither wanted nor needed response.

And yet she responded! Her body, despite two years of being asked to forget Ran's touch, forget Ran's very existence, seemed to blossom forth in desire. Her knees trembled; she would have fallen but for his hold on her, her pulse quickened in *desire*, not fear or even anger.

The heat of him seemed to burn through their clothing to sear her breasts, hardening her nipples against him. Her loins burned at the feel of him against her.

And he knew! As his mouth possessed her, he couldn't help but feel the betraying responses of her body. What remained of her consciousness ordered her hands to stay clenched at her sides; instead, they slowly lifted to grasp at his upper arms, revelling in the familiar touch of his hard muscles. Her thighs shifted closer to him, seeking the remembered touch of his strong, muscular legs.

Only Rena's eyes obeyed her; they stayed closed, unable to accept the sight of her former lover so close to her. But the rest of her body, like his, had no need of vision. As his lips became less demanding, more caressing, her own curved to meet them, tasting him, luxuriating in the taste of him.

When he released her arms to free his own hands for a more extensive exploration of her body, she unthinkingly raised them around his neck, her fingers entwined in the thickness of his hair. Her breasts quivered for his touch, demanding, crying out for the caress of his fingers. And when his lips moved away to run a trail of fire down her cheek, her throat, into the hollow of her shoulder, her own lips returned the caress along his jawline, kissing at his ear.

They fitted. Fitted as they always had; from the very first time Ran had ever kissed her, their bodies had seemed to know each other, to instinctively recognise exactly how to achieve the maximum closeness, the maximum sensation.

Rena flowed into him, all thought of resistance long gone, replaced now by a burning, consuming need of him. Her lips, her fingers, her very body strained for the essence of him, her voice cried out his name in silence.

And then it was over. So suddenly that Rena was taken completely by surprise, he recoiled from her, almost flinging her from him in a single violent movement.

'That'll do, I think,' he said, voice ragged. 'And now I think you'd better go.'

Rena was thunderstruck. What to say? What to do? Her entire being felt as if it had been wrenched apart, torn from that single essence it needed—Ran. She tried to speak, to see him through eyes blurred by tears.

'No!' he commanded. 'Not a word . . . not a single bloody feminine deceitful word. Just get out!'

And he turned away to grope his way towards the desk, flinging himself carelessly into his chair and then sitting, silent and still as a statue, his head in his hands.

'But . . .' She tried again, but no more words would come.

'I said get out. *Out*!' And his voice was as cold as the emptiness inside her.

She went. Not willingly, but in a blind rush of desperation that sent her hurtling through the doorway, down the stairs and out into the street, where she sat huddled in her car and cried, pouring out her soul to the emptiness of the night. It seemed hours before she was fit to drive, but still the black Jaguar hadn't come for Ran. Not that she cared.

Once home, she cried again, and this time the tears

were angry, bitter. Scalding tears that puffed up her eyes and burned tracks down her cheeks and into the pillow beneath her head. She hated Ran Logan more than she had ever done, even when he had left her. But what really hurt was the knowledge that she now hated herself even more.

When she finally got to sleep, it was the dulled, heavy sleep of emotional exhaustion, and she woke next day feeling as if she hadn't slept at all.

Numb, moving with the stilted, shambling movements of a zombie, she managed to get through the day. But only just. And not, she noticed, without drawing several concerned looks from the other girls at work. But no one asked, no one tried to infringe upon her privacy, and for this at least she was thankful.

The rest of the week and even the weekend followed much the same lines. Rena rose each morning feeling worse than when she had gone to bed, moved listlessly through the routines of shower and shampoo and dressing and breakfast, then drove to work and forced herself into the routine there. Each night, except for her regular singing gig, she drove home to a simple meal or none at all, and was in bed seeking desperately for sleep by nine o'clock.

She didn't go to class the next Wednesday. She did think about it, but every instinct, every remaining crumb of common sense within her, demanded that she stay away.

Would he have missed her? she wondered, but only in passing. Somehow it didn't seem likely. And how could it matter anyway? Ran must know her identity by this time; he surely couldn't have failed to recognise her kisses, her caresses. Even if his eyes told him nothing, his body—like hers—must have screamed in recognition.

But then maybe not. She had to keep reminding

herself that he probably didn't care that much in the
first place. Obviously, or he wouldn't have deserted
her the moment he had gained the prize he really
wanted. She puzzled over it all that evening, but went
to sleep without being any closer to really knowing.

Yet somehow the thinking helped, perhaps by virtue
of being the only really constructive thing she had done
in a week. She slept relatively well, and approached
her work the next morning feeling more or less normal
again.

Normal enough, surprisingly, that when her lunch
break arrived Rena found herself famished. But where
to go? She was strolling down the main street, mentally
assessing the counter lunch possibilities of the various
pubs, when she was hailed by a familiar voice.

'John,' she replied. 'How are you?'

'Fine,' replied her fellow creative writing student.
'And you seem a good deal better than was predicted
last night, I must say.'

'Last night?' She tried to be super-casual. 'What
could they have been predicting about me? That I'd
died or something?'

'No, nothing quite so drastic. Merely that you might
be ill or something, although I must say you don't look
ill to me. Louise, of course, held forth at some length
that you'd dropped out, but Logan wasn't having a bit
of that idea.'

John looked at her speculatively. 'He said you might
be all kinds of things, but he wouldn't believe you were
a quitter. I agreed with him, but now I'm not so sure.'

Rena didn't bother to try and hide her guilt. 'I think
perhaps you should have agreed with Louise,' she said
quietly.

John's grin was infectious. 'Ah well,' he said. 'I've
been wrong before; it won't kill me. I feel a bit sorry
for our esteemed teacher, though. He's going to look a

bit of a mug for having defended you so stoutly.'

Ran . . . defending her? Rena's incredulity must have been obvious.

'Find that hard to believe? My, my, you two really must have got off on the wrong foot,' said John, his pale blue eyes twinkling with amusement.

'I don't know what you mean by that,' Rena said.

'No, of course you don't,' he conceded blithely. 'You know, I may be getting on a bit, but unlike our esteemed teacher, I'm not blind. Nor stupid either,' he added.

Nor was he. Rena could see there wasn't much sense in pretending. 'That obvious?' she asked with a shy grin.

He laughed. 'Only to me, I think, but then I've a wealth of experience to draw on. But maybe to Louise as well, though I think she just doesn't like you because you're so much prettier.'

'You're an old flatterer!' But she was honestly pleased at the compliment and didn't try to hide it.

'And a dirty old man as well,' he replied. 'Unfortunately, just a bit too old for you, or Logan would find himself needing more than blindness as an advantage.'

Then his mood and tone changed abruptly. 'So you've quit, have you? Not just taken a week off to try and teach the lad a lesson?'

'I . . . don't see much to be gained by staying with it,' Rena hedged.

Old John's eyes were grim. Then he shrugged. 'Just as well, I suppose. Ran Logan isn't the type of man to play those kinds of games with, and if you ever expected to gain anything by it you'd be doomed to failure anyway. Seems a bit of a pity to give Louise such a clear field, though. She was all over him like a rash last night.'

Rena met his eyes directly, choking down the rush

of jealousy that boiled to life within her. 'And that's meant to make me jealous, I suppose,' she said. 'You've got a nerve, accusing *me* of playing games!'

John laughed. 'Really, my child, I have nothing to gain by making you jealous,' he said pointedly. 'Just giving you something to think about, that's all. Although I must admit I'd prefer to be taught by somebody in a better mood than I expect Logan might be if you weren't there. We'll just ignore the fact that Louise is a proper pain that will get worse as she goes along.'

Now it was Rena's turn to laugh. 'Why do I have the feeling you don't like the woman?' she chuckled. 'Personally I think she and Randall Logan would make an excellent pair. She's certainly very beautiful . . . you can't deny that.'

'All in the eye of the beholder,' John replied lazily, and Rena flinched at having her own words returned, however innocently. 'Besides,' he continued, 'young Logan isn't in much of a position to be impressed by all that redheaded pulchritude, is he?'

'What does that have to do with anything?' Rena was suspicious, and his next words confirmed her worst suspicions.

'Only that I think he already *knows* what you look like. And no, I don't expect you to admit it. Just a little private theory of my own, that's all.'

'You do have strange theories,' Rena replied, frantically searching for the right thing to say if she was to throw John as far from his *theory* as possible. 'Although he did say I had a voice that reminded him of someone; perhaps that's what set you off.'

'Whatever you say,' he replied laughingly, obviously not caring a whit whether she knew or not that he didn't believe her. 'Do you want me to tell him next week that you're out of it, then?'

'Yes!' The word formed in her mind, rattled around

on her tongue, but flatly refused to emerge. Rena stood there, knowing her mouth was moving, knowing she must look totally ridiculous to the canny, kindly older man facing her. But she could not say it.

John's laughter was loud, but not cruel. 'Should be an interesting class, I reckon,' he chortled. 'A teacher that can't see, one student that can't speak . . . perhaps I'll have to wear shorts and show off my wooden leg. Humph! I wonder what there is about Louise . . . besides congenital bitchiness, I mean? Maybe . . .' He patted himself on the chest. 'Well, just a thought.'

Just a thought, but one too many for Rena and for John as well. Oblivious to the curious stares of passers-by, they stood and howled with laughter, leaning on one another, finally, simply to keep from falling down.

It quite literally made Rena's day. She returned to work in a delightful frame of mind, happy and smiling and cheerful. It lasted until she got home that night to find a letter from her landlord—and Ran Logan's black Jaguar parked in front of the house.

CHAPTER FIVE

THE sight of the car was the worst shock of the two, at first. Rena nearly drove her own battered old machine through the back wall of the carport, she was so busy wondering how Ran had found her. And why.

But it wasn't Ran who emerged from the large, shiny car to meet Rena in front of her mailbox. It was Valerie Dunn, looking stunning and rather overdressed as usual. Also, Rena thought, looking somewhat out of sorts.

'Miss Everett? Yes, I suppose you must be,' said the

chic older woman, making no attempt to shake hands or be otherwise pleasant. 'I am Valerie Dunn, personal secretary to Mr Randall Logan.'

'Yes?' Only the one word. Rena didn't know—couldn't even imagine—what was going on, but she wasn't going to make anything easy for this woman she so deeply disliked.

'Frankly, I was rather expecting someone . . . older,' Valerie Dunn observed, obviously more concerned with her own ideas than anything Rena might have to say. 'You have put the flat in order, I presume.'

'Flat? I'm sorry, but I don't understand,' Rena replied, honestly confused and not really in the mood to play guessing games.

'Well, of course, the flat,' Miss Dunn said crossly, waving a general flick of one perfectly-manicured hand towards Rena's house. Then she paused, her face angry and cross.

What came next was a single, surprisingly crude expletive, a word not at all in keeping with the woman's carefully-tended appearance and sophistication. Rena stayed silent, inwardly quite enjoying Valerie Dunn's loss of composure. More than just enjoyable, she thought. There was a certain savage satisfaction.

'I suppose you've not received the letter . . . don't know what I'm talking about at all,' Valerie spat. 'Typical . . . just typical!' She then launched into a vicious condemnation of the Australian postal service—particularly the Queensland portion thereof.

Rena didn't bother to listen; instead she moved the few steps necessary and reached into her letter box to collect the usual selection of junk mail and, surprisingly, a letter from her landlord.

To her surprise, Valerie pounced on the letter, almost grabbing it from Rena's very fingers once she'd seen the letterhead on the envelope.

'Hah! Just as I thought,' she cried. Then, in tones that clearly delineated her expectations of Rena's position in the whole matter, 'Perhaps you'd like to read that—now—so that I can conclude my business here and get back to my proper duties.'

For a moment Rena seriously considered refusal. It would, she thought, serve the haughty bitch right. But to put her off would only mean having to face her yet again, presumably. There couldn't be any question that Valerie Dunn knew what the letter contained, even if Rena didn't.

Which, Rena thought, was all the more confusing. And, somehow . . . threatening. What possible connection was there?

Ah well, only one way to find out, she thought. And ripped open the envelope, though not without first steeling herself for a shock. And just as well she did!

Her landlord, it seemed, wouldn't be coming north this winter. His wife wasn't up to it. But a friend of his, one Randall Logan by name, was apparently in Bundaberg 'on some wild goose chase or another' and was finding his present accommodation quite unsatisfactory. Naturally, having been told this in passing while the two men were discussing something quite irrelevant to the current issue, her landlord had thought it only proper to offer his flat to an old and trusted friend. Mr Logan's secretary, Miss Dunn, would be calling to ensure this didn't cause Rena any problems, and if for any reason it did, Rena was to telephone him directly.

Problems? Rena could have screamed. She stood and read the letter again and again, almost oblivious to Valerie Dunn's impatient figure beside her.

Problems? It would mean worse than just problems. It would mean . . . well, *big* problems. And yet what could she do about it? Rena could just imagine her landlord's reaction to any sort of excuses she might concoct. Even the truth would seem beyond belief, not that she'd dare tell him that in the first place.

But to have Ran here, living in the same house, having to see him regularly? And even worse, having Valerie Dunn here as well, having to know, to see, what they shared ... Rena shook her head, flinging her mane of sable hair in a gesture that could have meant anything, but to her meant simply defeat.

'I'll get you the keys,' she said dully. And not even the woman's officious, patronising, demanding attitude could penetrate the dull, nagging start of a headache that had its beginnings not in Rena's head, but in her heart.

Valerie Dunn, fortunately, didn't stay long. Only enough to glance disparagingly round the simply-furnished ground floor flat, her every attitude suggesting she thought it entirely unsuitable.

'Well, I suppose it has at least the advantage of sea breezes,' she finally condescended.

'That can be more important than you'd expect, especially in summer,' Rena replied, feeling almost conscience-bound to defend this lower, seldom used portion of what she thought of as *her* home. 'But then perhaps you won't be staying that long.'

'God knows!' The woman's reply was almost a derisive snort. 'If I had my way we wouldn't be here at all, but...' Then, as if realising she had perhaps already said too much, she clamped her perfectly-painted mouth shut.

'I wasn't meaning to pry,' Rena said graciously. A graciousness she certainly didn't feel. She *hadn't* been meaning to pry, but in retrospect she dearly wished she'd got a more comprehensive answer.

Even more interesting, she thought after Valerie Dunn had departed and Rena was alone in her own

flat, would have been some suggestion about why
Ran Logan had come north in the first place. Not
knowing that, it was difficult even to speculate on
how long he might be staying. At least six weeks
more, though, assuming he would finish the course
he had begun.

Six weeks . . . a lifetime in some respects and hardly
anything at all in others, she thought. And wondered
if, by some freak chance, Ran *knew* he'd be flatting in
the same house as herself.

The answer came, from Rena's viewpoint, nowhere
near quickly enough. Despite Valerie Dunn's vague
suggestion that the move would take place 'in a day or
so', it was late Saturday afternoon before Rena saw the
black Jaguar again. And this time the elegant female
driver wasn't alone.

What to do? Rena caught her first glimpse of the car
from her kitchen window; there was nothing but the
presence of her own vehicle in one half of the carport
to suggest she might be home. Dared she simply ignore
their arrival? Or should she play good neighbour and
see them safely settled?

Cowardice won. She cursed herself for a prying,
spineless busybody, but merely established a surrepti-
tious watching brief as case after case was unloaded
from the big car.

At one point she nearly *did* go down, but wisely
thought twice about it. She knew it would only end in
disaster if she were to complain about Ran being left
sitting in a hot, confining motor car while his secretary
gave first priority to the movement of her own luggage.

But once the luggage, and finally Ran, was in the
flat below, things took on an oppressive silence. It was
smothering, bothersome, like the build-up to a thun-
derstorm. And after less than an hour, during which

the subtropical darkness dropped like a shroud, Rena
knew she couldn't take any more.

Abandoning her original plans for an early night
with a light supper and some time spent washing her
hair, she threw on a pair of jeans and a light jacket,
then crept silently down the outside staircase and
strode off down the esplanade in steps quickened by
her nervous tension.

Gradually, as she walked southward beyond the
built-up esplanade area and on to a rutted gravel track
that paralleled the sea, the soft swishing of waves
calmed her, slowed her steps. The rising moon made it
quite light enough to walk in safety, and Rena just
kept on heading south.

She walked for hours, down past the old quarry,
along the scrubby heathland to where a narrow creek
died within reach of the sea itself at this dry time of
year, and finally on to the glistening sands of Mon
Repos, world famous as a turtle rookery and one of the
district's major tourist attractions. Then back again,
retracing her steps homeward.

She approached the now dark house with slow, silent
steps, not wishing to wake anyone. It was, she realised
without the need for a watch, somewhat later than she
had originally thought; almost all of the Oaks' houses
were already dark.

Ran's Jaguar was now parked in the carport beside
her own ageing machine, moonlight recoiling from
their flanks. She glanced at the broad, lower-floor verandah, shaded by her own balcony above, but saw no
one. Hardly unexpected, she thought, until she reached
the bottom of the staircase and heard her own name
whispered softly.

At first she didn't believe it, thinking it a trick of the
night wind, but when she paused the whisper was
repeated and her startled eyes finally found the source.

'Why are you sitting out here in the middle of the night?' she whispered in reply. Forgotten was her week-and-a-half-old anger; now she felt only surprise and concern.

'Enjoying the peace and quiet,' he chuckled. 'And the surprises. I knew the other tenant of this place was named Everett, but I hardly expected it to be you.'

'No,' she replied hesitantly, suspicion returning with the memory of their last encounter. 'No, I suppose you wouldn't.'

'I'll bet *you* were surprised, though,' he chuckled, louder this time. 'I understand you didn't get much warning about all this.'

Rena didn't reply. Indeed, what could she say? That if she had been given warning she'd have found some way to object? That she wished he weren't here? It was senseless to reply; it was too late for anything she might think to make the slightest bit of difference.

'You weren't amused by me coming here.' Not quite a question, but not really a statement; it demanded some form of reply.

'It's none of my business,' she said.

'You were *not* amused.' This time it was a flat statement. Too, the chuckle was gone from his voice, replaced by a tone mingling bitterness with regret.

'I didn't say that,' she replied quite unnecessarily, and got the expectable reply.

'You didn't have to. I don't need my eyes to tell me that.'

'All right, I wasn't amused,' she snapped. 'But since I don't have much choice in the matter, I certainly can't see much sense in arguing about it.'

'You could have screamed for help to Bob Jacobsen. I was quite specific when I talked to him . . . not wanting to put anybody out.'

'You're not about to put me *out*,' she retorted. 'I

don't see that having you here is going to make any difference to me at all, unless you persist in skulking about like a thief in the night and frightening hell out of me!'

His laugh this time was so loud that she shushed him. 'You'll wake Miss ... whatever her name is,' Rena cautioned, not wanting to be found in this particular circumstance by the super-efficient Miss Dunn.

'I wouldn't worry about it,' he replied. And was there still bitterness in his voice ... or something else entirely? 'She sleeps like the dead.'

'Well, I suppose you'd know.' And she paused, mouth still open in surprise. Had she really said *that*? Thought it, certainly, but surely she hadn't actually ... not out loud ...

'My, my, my, is that a bit of the old green-eyed monster I detect?' His words removed all doubt. 'Funny, I wouldn't have thought you the dog-in-the-manger type, Rena.' Ran's voice was alive now, vibrant with sarcasm but not loud enough to disturb anyone.

'Frankly, I don't much care what you think,' she snapped. 'Besides, you don't know enough about me to make such judgments.'

'And never will,' he finished for her, solemnly. 'But I think I know more about you than you'd expect. You've no idea how blindness heightens the other senses—like touch, for example.'

'And rudeness! Not to mention conceit,' she snorted. 'I think you just use it as an excuse for pawing anything female that comes within reach.'

'You know better than that, although I don't expect you to admit it,' he replied calmly. 'And regardless of what you might say now, you certainly didn't mind being kissed by me last week.'

True. Too true! What she had minded was the betrayal by her own body, her own heart. But to admit that would be the first step to total disaster. She said nothing.

'Does my blindness upset you so much?' he asked after a brief silence.

Upset her? And yet how could she tell him how much, how it tore at her heart to see him that way?

'Not ... in the way I think you mean,' she replied honestly enough.

'You mean you're not physically repulsed by it, I suppose,' he mused, almost idly. 'Which I rather think I must interpret to mean that you dislike me then just because I'm a man; the blindness isn't really a signifi-cant factor. Did he hurt you all *that* badly, then?'

'Who?'

'You know damned well who ... or whom ... I mean. This fellow who seems to have managed to put you off men for life. I'd like to have met him when I could see; perhaps I'd have hammered some sense into his thick head.'

Rena choked back an hysterical giggle, choked it back and had to keep swallowing convulsively to hold it from escaping. The thought of Ran thumping *himself* over the head was simply too much for her fragile emotions.

Ran, however, appeared to take her silence as something quite different. 'I don't suppose you think it might help to talk about it?' he enquired gently. 'I've become quite a good listener, in recent times.'

Tell him about it? Tell *him*? But then why not? Wasn't that one thing she'd been wanting to do for two long years? To meet Randall Logan face to face and tell him what a bastard he was? Of course it was, only she hadn't calculated on finding him blind. And she knew she couldn't attack him—personally—be-cause of that damnable factor.

'All right,' she said. 'He met me; he seduced me; he

left me. That's about all there is to it.'

'I'm sure it's a good deal more complicated than that, but I certainly share your feelings,' he replied. 'I suppose you loved him?'

'Of course not,' she replied scathingly. 'I hop into bed with every man I meet and then get horribly emotional afterwards.'

'Which means he was the first ... and presumably the last man you've been to bed with,' he replied with astonishing accuracy. 'And a fair time ago, judging from your reaction to me last week.'

'I think you tend to put far too much faith in what you think you feel,' Rena snapped.

'Well, you didn't immediately hop into bed with me, as you so arrogantly put it,' he replied. 'So it's obvious the fellow taught you one lesson, at least.'

Rena caught herself before her hand reached out instinctively to strike him. She wouldn't do that again; she knew his concept of retaliation too well.

'Yes, I suppose you could certainly say that,' she agreed. Damn him! He certainly *could* say that! But why then was there so little satisfaction in the fact that he couldn't even see the truth of his own words?

'What did he do ... for a living, I mean?' A casual enough question, but it sent warning signals through Rena's mind. But after a pause, she answered him truthfully.

'A journalist ... that'd be right,' he muttered. 'I know the type only too well.'

Too, too well, Rena thought, and almost smiled at the irony of it. What would he do, she wondered, if she dropped all pretence and told him the plain, unvarnished truth? If only he weren't blind ... but she couldn't, not this way. Instead, she resorted to scorn.

'And I suppose you're going to tell me now that you're so much different?' she scoffed.

As well scoff at the wind. When he finally replied it was in a voice so calm, so cool, that she wondered if he had even felt the scorn.

'Perhaps not. Although I suppose he must have told you he loved you. I've never done that just to get a girl into my bed.'

Liar! The word screamed into her mind so vividly that for an instant she thought she had screamed it aloud. But she hadn't; not even super-cool Ran Logan could take that charge without a change of expression.

'And I suppose next you'll tell me you've never had to,' she sneered.

'I've only ever once in my life told a woman I loved her—and I meant it,' he replied quietly, expressionlessly. 'Which isn't to say I might not do it again . . . some day.'

'That isn't what I meant,' Rena replied, her mouth revealing the confusion in her mind. He'd sounded so sincere, so totally honest . . . but he wasn't. She knew that; she was the living, breathing evidence of his deceit.

'Love isn't the only reason two people go to bed together,' he replied. 'And if you're fishing for numbers or whatever, forget it.'

'Why? Don't tell me you've lost count?' her voice was syrup-sweet, but the syrup was poisoned, bitter as almond even in her own mouth.

'Don't be crude. I offered to be a sounding board, not a wall for you to bounce your bitterness off.' He sounded bored.

'I think it's time I went in,' she replied. This was getting too intense, too close to the pains inside her.

'Maybe we should change the subject, instead,' he said. 'Are you going to come back to classes, or have you washed your hands of that, too?'

Was she? Certainly it didn't make sense to avoid him

one night a week when he was living virtually in her pocket.

'I . . . don't know for certain,' she hedged.

'I'm perfectly willing to apologise for last week. I'll even say please.' He was smiling now, teeth glinting in the soft, pale moonlight.

'Don't bother.' She sounded short with him, but she knew it was herself she was out of tune with.

'Oh, but I must,' he grinned. 'Although not without an ulterior motive; you'd expect that, of course. I was merely thinking it might be convenient for us to travel together.'

'I'm sure your secretary would like that,' Rena countered.

'She probably would, but in actual fact I'm thinking of sending her back to Sydney. She really cannot abide life up here; it isn't her scene at all.'

'But . . . but how would you cope? I mean, living out here, and alone . . . it's sort of isolated, you know.'

'So am I . . . so am I,' he drawled wearily. 'What the hell difference does it make, in the long run? At least out here I can smell the sea, taste the salt in the air. It's better than the awful stink of sugar cane being processed.'

'Almost anything is,' Rena agreed drily. 'But I'd be careful about saying so, if I were you. Up here, that's the smell of money.'

'I'd have expected you to be used to it, having lived here all your life.' Again he bespoke her own lies, and it hurt. Rena shivered. She would have thought so too, but the road to and from Bundaberg led straight past— and downwind of—Qunaba Mill, which made each day's drive on the Bundaberg Port road an olfactory nightmare. The sickly sweet scent of the crushed sugar might be the smell of money, but it was anything but pleasant.

'Yes, but ... but what about cooking ... and ... well, just everything?' she queried, returning to her original point. The thought of leaving Ran stranded and alone was incomprehensible. What kind of woman was this secretary of his?

'Oh, I daresay I'll manage,' he shrugged. 'Blind people aren't nearly as handicapped as some people imagine ... at least in some respects.'

'That isn't the point and you know it,' she replied hotly, her voice probably revealing her displeasure at the insanity of the proposal. She didn't care; it was ludicrous and she fully intended he should know it. 'What are you going to do all day, for instance? The bus service is only a school service; there's a long walk even just to the pub ... oh, it's ... it's just ridiculous!'

He merely shrugged, untouched by her concerns. 'I don't need the pub—there's a phone here in case of emergency; and if I need to go anywhere I can always call a taxi. What's the hassle? Or is it that you're afraid you'll be stuck with looking after me?'

'That wasn't what I meant at all.' But it was, although he wasn't to know the true basis for her worry on that score. To look after him, to cook his meals, organise his clothing, just ... be with him. That would be the purest combination of heaven and hell she could imagine.

'I'm glad, because one of the reasons Valerie is going back to Sydney is that I'm damned well sick and tired of being fussed over,' he snarled. His voice was a throaty growl that left no room for doubt. He meant it. Rena felt a strange lightness in her heart, which raced wildly just at the words. No Valerie Dunn. But then no Rena, either. Not really ...

'Well, I think it's a bit stupid,' she said. 'Not that it's any of my business, of course ...'

'Of course. Except on Wednesday nights, if you

decide to combine the roles of student and chauffeur. It'll be your business then, because I'll insist on taking you to dinner first, so you'll have to be ready to check that my tie's straight and I haven't got on mismatched socks.'

She giggled; she couldn't help it. It was simply impossible to imagine the Ran Logan she knew with a crooked tie or mismatched socks.

'On second thoughts, maybe we'd best forget it,' he said then—bitterly. 'It strikes me you'd think it hilarious to see me out in public with mismatched socks or soup stains all over my tie.'

'That's not fair!' Rena's indignation almost made her shout, and she quickly lowered her voice. 'That's a hateful thing to say about anyone!'

'*Anyone* wouldn't have giggled at the thought,' Ran replied without retracting. 'Although . . .' and he paused as if for thought, 'I really wouldn't have thought you a vengeful woman, although I can't imagine why.'

'I'm not!' And that, she decided, was no lie. If she were a vengeful woman, would she even be here? Would she have suppressed her own feelings of betrayal and hurt just to keep from taking advantage of his infirmity?

'Just a manhater,' he said almost musingly. 'And you won't tell me why. Or not *really* why, to be specific. Now if you'd been through what I have . . . no, we'll ignore that. But I have to say, even knowing you'll reject it anyway, that it's not quite fair to judge all men by the misdeeds of one.'

'Do you think I don't know that?' she asked, not really wanting an answer. She didn't judge all men by one—just Ran Logan by Ran Logan. And the evidence was damning!

'Oh, I think you know it . . . intellectually,' he said.

'But in the heart, that's something else again.' He smiled, but it was the smile of a dangerous, hunting animal. 'I know a bit about that myself, since my accident.'

'You never did tell me about your accident,' she said, praying inwardly that he wouldn't sense the desperate need in her to know, to know every single detail. 'Not . . . not that it's any of my business, of course, and if you'd rather not . . .'

He shrugged aside her hesitations. 'Nothing much to tell, really. I got involved in covering a small riot, didn't watch my back carefully enough, and got smacked over the head with something. When I came out of it, I was blind. Also pretty severely concussed and a bit cut and bruised, but the blindness was obviously the greatest concern.'

'I see.' Which was a lie; she didn't see at all. 'But didn't you say it was only . . . temporary?'

'Well, that's what the doctors thought, and that's what I thought . . . until it happened again. Now they say it's psychosomatic and I . . . honestly don't know. It's here, anyway.'

Oh, damn you, Ran Logan, she thought. There's more to this than you're telling and I can't appear *too* curious. Why won't you just tell me *everything*?

'It . . . it must have been horrible for you,' she said, shuddering at how patronising and expectable the remark must sound.

'Oh, the first time wasn't too bad,' he said with a quite unexpected grin. 'I was out cold for most of the time anyway, and when I did start to come good I managed to get a good deal of comfort from everyone's assertions that the blindness really was only temporary.'

'But what caused the second blindness . . . or relapse, or whatever?' she asked. 'Did you have another accident, or . . .?'

'No, nothing like that,' he said. 'I came back to Australia feeling quite fit, all thing considered. Oh, the
occasional headache, that sort of thing, but my eyes
were fine. And then . . . well, something happened that,
let's just say rather thoroughly destroyed my faith in
w . . . human nature. I don't understand the medical
aspects of it all, but the blindness returned gradually
then and I've been stuck with it ever since.'

Rena couldn't help but catch his faltering over the
term human nature, and—unfortunately—couldn't
help her mouth running away with her good sense.

'I gather your human nature was of the female variety?' she asked in a tone that was blunt despite the
shakiness of her own emotions.

Ran shook his head sadly and grimaced. 'My word,
but you're observant,' he retorted sarcastically. 'Yes, I
was led down the proverbial garden path, as I must
presume you were. The only difference in my case is
that my blindness appears to have been the cause. My
original blindness, that is.'

He sighed, deeply and with that soul-wrenching
futility of betrayal that Rena knew only too well. 'I
suppose,' he said, 'it's that part which hurts most. I
could have understood being . . . dumped just . . . as
it happens. But not because of something like
that.'

Rena gasped. She simply couldn't comprehend this!
Bad enough to be faced with the fact that Ran had, to
use his own words, dumped *her* for someone else. But
to have done it for a woman who would then turn
around and abandon him when he needed her most . . .

'I . . . I'm sorry,' she said. And meant it, more than
he must ever be allowed to understand.

'Don't be!' His retort was harsh, brittle. Cruel, even.
'I certainly wouldn't apologise for mankind in general
for what happened to you, and I don't need either

sympathy or misplaced apologies for my own problems.'

Then he grinned, again that horrible wolfish grin
that disguised so much bitterness, so much pain, that
Rena shuddered. 'Besides, I was warned. So I guess
I've only myself to blame in any event.'

'Warned? Do you mean she ... she ...?' Rena
simply couldn't bring herself to complete the question.
Valerie Dunn—now she was a woman Rena could
imagine uttering such a warning. But obviously it
hadn't been Valerie Dunn, who was still very much in
evidence. And who else ... what else, what kind of
cruel, unfeeling woman might do such a thing?

'If you mean did she warn me in advance that she
couldn't face life with a blind man, no,' he replied
coldly, almost angrily. 'She wouldn't have had the guts
to be that honest, apparently. But she made it clear
enough to ... someone ... after the fact.'

'I ... I can't imagine such a thing,' Rena said. 'I
just can't imagine it. You're saying she didn't even
hang about until the diagnosis was confirmed—as it
wouldn't have been, from what you've said?'

'That's about the size of it,' he growled. 'From what
I understand she found out I was blinded, asked very
few questions at all, but quite quickly and conveniently
disappeared.'

'My ... God!' Rena breathed.

'Oh, don't sound so astounded,' he snarled. 'I'm
sure you know as well as I do that such things happen.'

'Obviously,' she replied drily, rather piqued by his
attitude. 'It happened to me, too, remember? Although
at least I wasn't blinded as you were.' Not blinded,
but surely blind, she thought. And equally vulnerable,
shouted some demon inside her. You might have been
pregnant!

'No, but you might have ended up with an equally difficult burden. You could have found yourself pregnant.' Ran's voice echoed that of the demon inside, and Rena shivered at the truth of a fear she had quite forgotten having experienced.

'It's hardly the same thing,' she snapped, unaccountably irritated by his remark. 'I'm quite sure you weren't personally involved in your eventual blindness.'

'That isn't what the doctors say,' he replied with a hint of wry grin playing about his mouth. 'According to them, don't forget, I'm not blind at all—except in my head. And if you mean the lady in question wasn't personally involved, well . . . maybe not.'

'I don't think I follow you.'

Ran shrugged, almost as if he was now bored by it all. 'I didn't become blind, the second time, until I was faced with the irrefutable evidence that she'd . . . pulled the pin, as it were. That's why the quacks reckon it's all psychosomatic—some kind of reaction to the shock of having been deserted.'

'You must have loved her very much,' Rena said, denying the demons that cried out how often he'd claimed to love *her*, too.

'Nothing I won't get over . . . in time.' But he *had* loved this mysterious, cold-hearted bitch, Rena could tell. It was written all over him, in the calculated casualness, the wry, ironic twists of his lip, the bitter coldness that occasionally flared forth. Oh, why, she wondered, couldn't he have loved *her* like that? She would have stood by him.

Certainly better, she thought, than he had stood by her. And she fell silent, wallowing in her own silent, unspeakable bitterness, until he broke the silence himself.

'Does it make you feel any better to find out you're

not the only victim in the game, Rena?' His voice was changed, now, somehow softer, more gentle, compelling.

'Should it?' she snapped, 'I never thought for a minute that I was the first—or last—to be taken in by a smooth line.'

'No, I suppose not. But tell me, what would you do now, if you could meet this fellow face to face and have it out with him?'

It was too close to home. Too personal. Too ... unanswerable under the circumstances.

'What would you do?' she countered in a desperate bid to gain thinking time.

'I'm not sure, but one day I'll find out,' he replied calmly. 'There was a time when I'm quite certain I'd have killed the bitch.'

And he meant it: no question of that in Rena's mind. He must have been ... as hurt and bewildered and angry as was she herself. But to say now that one day he'd find out ... she couldn't resist the question.

'I know you'll think I'm being callous, but how will you know her if you do find her?' she asked, trembling a bit inside as she awaited his reply.

His answer was totally unexpected, and therefore impossible for her avoid. One lean hand reached out to grasp her own with unerring accuracy, lifting it, holding it to his lips for a kiss that burned like acid, then dropping it before she could even think to object.

'Oh, I fancy I'll know her right enough,' he said in a voice so cold, so deadly cold, that she shuddered. 'After all, I seem to find it easy enough to recognise you without seeing you. Don't I?'

'Well, so you think,' she replied with a confidence she didn't feel. 'I imagine that given half a dozen women with my perfume and general size and you wouldn't find it so easy.'

Ran's laugh was low and gurgling with suppressed merriment. Quite unexpected, considering how serious he'd been only moments before.

'And think how much more difficult it would be if I could see again,' he chuckled. 'Especially if all six were beautiful; I'd have the devil's own time choosing then, wouldn't I?'

'Be serious,' Rena snapped, glad he couldn't see the blush that had climbed up from the hollow of her breasts to flow across her throat and cheeks.

Instead, he reached out to take her fingers again in his own, and while she was wondering how he could possibly—in his blindness—be so damnably accurate, he replied: 'But what could be more serious? Do you realise that I don't know at all what you look like ... that my entire conception is based on a voice and a general idea of size? And of course, the way you kiss.'

And once again he drew her hand up, touching it with his lips in exactly the manner he *used* to do that, so very long ago when he had said he loved her, when she had loved him. His lips were a slow, deliberate instrument of torture, moving across the back of her hand, then across her palm as he turned her defenceless wrist, then on to her wrist itself, firing her pulse to improbably racing, pounding life.

Her mind screamed. Her heart, beneath its pounding, cried out in desperation. But the muscles that tensed to yank her hand from his grasp were limp, useless. Control of her body flowed across to him like electrical current through a wire.

'Don't.' Was it a whisper, or merely the sound of her mind inside her brain? 'Please don't.' That was her voice; even she heard it, but if Ran heard he made no acknowledgement.

He came to his feet, sliding erect in one sinuous, easy movement and drawing her unprotesting body with him. His lips never left her wrist, never ceased to hold her with an hypnotic, claiming certainty.

As Rena flowed into his arms, her lips rising to meet his mouth as it flowed up her arm, across the hollow of her shoulder, her mind screamed at the folly. But her body obeyed, obeying not her own cries for salvation, but the insistent, persuasive aura of Ran's presence.

And then she was in his arms, her body moulded to his, her heaving breasts against the strong, flexing muscles of his chest, her lips softly merging with his own, her thighs taut against the tautness of his thighs. She couldn't breathe, her mind was a soundless, airless vacuum, her body a rag doll in his hands.

His mouth was a magnet, claiming her lips, drawing their softness, giving life to them. His arms went round her, his fingers closing in the hollow of her back for an instant before embarking upon an exploration of tantalising, fingertip expertise. She felt his fingers in the softness above her trouser waist, along the nubbly knuckles of her spine, rising to where bra-line would have been if she had been wearing one.

Then they moved lower, kneading into the softness at the base of her spine, each delicate fingertip alive in itself, rousing her, drawing her closer to him, spreading vibrations of love, of life itself.

His mouth softened on her lips, melding the tastes of them both as his lips softened hers, making her mouth more pliant, more biddable to his will.

Rena's knees turned to jelly; had he not been holding her she would have fallen. Her stomach fluttered in gyrations of ecstasy; her fingers trembled as they brushed against the nape of his neck, feeling the coarseness of his hair, the hotness of his skin. Wherever he touched her, she was loose, alive with his vibrant physical essense.

Her mind screamed in protest. This was wrong! This

was folly, a deadly foolishness that could only bring more pain, more heartbreak, more suffering. But her body rejoiced; this was right, this was heaven itself.

When his fingertips flowed down across the taut hollows of her tummy, down to the softness beneath her waistband, she could only sigh her pleasure, her lips whispering meaningless delights.

But she was not entirely abandoned. When his fingers touched at the waistband of her jeans she shrank away; when they became more insistent she murmured her objections.

Forget that her fingers were now buried in the hair of his chest; forget that the open buttons of his shirt-front were open because she had opened them, her fingers flicking like wildfire across the buttons to let his body come even closer to her. Forget that she hated him, loved him, despised him and cherished his touch. This was right and wrong and perfect all at once.

She wanted him, her body cried out for him, her mind was a mere annoyance with cries for common sense, for restraint. Too late now for restraint as her fingers flowed down across the muscled smoothness of his stomach, down against the hard maleness of him, the essence of him for which her body cried so loudly in desire.

Holding her, he leaned back, sliding his body clumsily on to the length of the porch swing on which he had been sitting. Rena went with him, her mind protesting and her body moving to help him, to balance him, to position them both on the softness of the cushions.

His weight shifted to slide her into position, his hands already busy at the waist of her jeans and her own fingers drinking in the pleasure of him as her hips shifted to aid his explorations. The swing creaked as it took their weight, then groaned in protest as the imbalance caught, tipping them downward in a welter of limbs and falling metal framework.

CHAPTER SIX

'RANDALL? What's happened? Are you all right?'

The voice seemed right beside them, an extension of the light that suddenly blazed into being within the flat.

Rena cried out—silently—as she swarmed to her feet, scrabbling against the tiled deck of the verandah as she scurried like a small frightened animal towards the base of the stairs. In seconds she was up them, creeping silently but swiftly on all fours, her heart pounding in her heaving breast and Ran's 'get out of it' whisper still loud in her ears.

'It's all right, for God's sake,' came his voice, behind her now. Ran's voice, astonishingly calm, astonishingly clear in the sudden stillness. 'I just slipped and knocked over the porch swing, that's all.'

More light, this time from the porch flood as Valerie Dunn emerged from the front door, wrapping a flimsy, almost sheer nightgown around her. She was like a magazine model, not a hair out of place, not a single sleep-smudge around her deep-set green eyes.

Rena cowered in her own little pool of shadow at the top of the stairs, afraid to move, now, lest she be heard. Afraid not to move, lest she be seen.

'Randall . . . you're impossible!' the auburn-haired woman exclaimed. 'Just look at you . . . and of course sitting out here alone in the middle of the night. What am I to do with you?'

'Exactly as you've always done, I should imagine,'

Ran replied. Rather wearily, Rena thought, as if this were a discussion of long standing between him and his exquisite secretary. 'Why don't you trot off back to bed, Valerie? I'm quite all right, as you can see.'

'If you were quite all right,' came the reply in sultry but officious tones, 'we wouldn't be here in this ridiculous little backwater in the first place. We'd be in Sydney, where you can have proper medical help on tap as you need it, and where I can take care of you properly.'

Ran snorted. 'The fact that the place would drive me mad being quite irrelevant to the issue, I suppose?'

His secretary shifted closer to him, her bare arms winding round him, Rena thought, like two silky smooth snakes. Vipers. 'Poor darling,' she cooed, lips moving up to brush at his cheek. 'Why can't you give up this obsession of yours and let's go back to civilisation? You won't find what you're looking for here, no matter how long you stay.'

'That,' he retorted steadfastly, 'is a matter of some considerable opinion. Anyway, I'm stuck with the place now until this course is finished and there's no way around that.'

Valerie Dunn grimaced. 'That course! Really, Randall . . . it wasn't one of your better decisions to take on such a project. I thought you'd have realised that by now.'

'Oh, I don't know. I'm quite enjoying it,' he replied. 'More than I expected, certainly. Much more.'

'Yes, but what about your own writing? You've done virtually nothing since we arrived,' the woman replied. She was still pasted against Ran, and Rena was chagrined to notice he made no attempt whatsoever to pull away.

Damn him! He knew perfectly well she was watching, knew she was poised like a burglar at the top of the stairs. How could he possibly force her to watch such a performance after the lovemaking they had just shared?

'My own writing isn't suffering,' he replied casually, one arm sliding out to wrap itself about the woman's slender waist in a gesture that made Rena's heart seeth with white hate. She fairly writhed with her anger as the woman insinuated herself within the circle of Ran's arm—an arm that only minutes before had been circled around Rena's own even more slender waist.

Valerie Dunn's throaty chuckle was like a purr of pleasure, but Rena could see—if Ran could not—the true expression of long-suffering patience on the woman's face. She was shocked at such obvious duplicity; surely Ran could tell that he was simply being used for some selfish purpose by his secretary?

Rena couldn't hear what Valerie said next, because it was whispered into Ran's only-too-willing ear. She could do nothing but stay in her place and wonder as the two people below her shifted to the doorway and finally went inside.

When the door had closed and the lights went out to plunge the outside of the two-storey house into stygian darkness, Rena sat huddled like some gargoyle, unwilling to move, unable to trust the holocaust of emotion within her.

Certainly what came next was obvious enough. Her eyes had seen the evidence in Valerie Dunn's sinuous approaches. If Ran were to suffer any withdrawal symptoms from having his lovemaking interrupted, it wouldn't be for lack of effort on his secretary's part to solve the problem.

And for Rena? Certainly she had no opportunity to salve her own trembling body's physical needs, much less the far more important mental conflicts that threatened her. How could Ran do such a thing?

Couldn't he see—blind or not—that he was being used?

Or, said the demon voice of pure jealousy within her, did he *see* it only too well, but consider it a small price to pay for the gratification of his physical needs and a means to punish Rena for . . . for what? She had done nothing, except to let her damnably treacherous body once more take command of its own destiny.

When she finally crept silently into her own flat, moving with infinite caution and cursing herself for the guilt she felt—although how much *more* guilty, she wondered, to have been surprised by Valerie Dunn a few minutes later?—at allowing herself to succumb to the temptations of Ran Logan yet again.

'You're a fool, Catherine Conley Everett,' she whispered to herself once she had gained the lonely sanctuary of her own bed. 'A blind, stupid, gullible fool. At least Valerie Dunn may get some benefit out of letting Ran Logan use her—you get nothing but more pain, more heartache.'

It was obvious enough, but it did nothing to solve the even more obvious problem. Rena loved Ran Logan, had never stopped loving him despite his betrayal, and would go on loving him despite his totally callous disregard for her and her feelings.

She glanced at her bedside clock just before drifting off into a troubled sleep, and was surprised to find it was only just past midnight. Six hours later the first rays of sub-tropical sunshine peeped through her window, demanding to be noticed and consistently oblivious to her need to sleep.

Sunday; a day of rest. But how to rest, when inside her mind a kaleidoscope of images whirled in frenetic circles to prick annoyingly at her most base emotions— jealousy, anger, hatred. And fear. Fear that she could never, ever, come to terms with herself and the influence Ran Logan had held—would hold—in her life.

She showered, washed her long hair and conditioned it, ate what was, for her, a hearty breakfast. And every second of the time her mind was obsessed with Ran . . . her ears cocked for any sound of life, of movement in the flat below. She fought off mental visions of what must have happened after Ran and Valerie had re-entered their flat the evening before.

Fought them off, but not for long and not completely enough to alleviate her own cravings, her own inner tensions. It was one thing, in the cold light of dawn, to intellectually theorise that Ran had only played up to Valerie to divert the woman's attention. But quite another to deny the green-eyed monster of jealousy within Rena herself.

How could she possibly survive another month and a half of Ran's presence? She wouldn't, she realised only too well, be able to avoid him entirely. If nothing else, she must see him, be in close contact with him, each Wednesday evening. It would be pointless and silly to give up the writing classes in the existing circumstances.

But none of this solved the problem of today and what to do with it. She must get away from the house; perhaps a drive, an afternoon touring the various art galleries, a long, solitary stroll along the beach? None appealed, and yet her logic told her she couldn't possibly stay home, not with the likelihood of having to face Ran yet again, and this time probably Valerie Dunn as well.

In any event, it was too early to go anywhere if it meant taking her aged car. The shuddering, coughing roar of it starting up would be guaranteed to wake up those below, so Rena sat herself at the kitchen table and tried to concentrate on some new songs she was working up for her Monday night gigs.

That, at least, seemed to help her troubled mind. Within half an hour she was so deeply immersed in the exercise that at first she didn't even hear the argument which had begun on the floor below. It wasn't until Valerie Dunn said loudly, 'But that's totally absurd!' that Rena pricked up her ears.

'I don't see what's so absurd about it.' Ran's voice, that rich, melodious voice she knew so well. 'You don't like it here, and there's no sense in denying it. I'm not helpless, as you very well know. And besides, with this Everett girl living right upstairs, I don't see the hassle.'

'The Everett girl, I might remind you, has to work for a living,' snapped Valerie. 'Every day, which means you'd be quite alone here during the day.'

'Which would suit me right down to the ground,' Ran replied implacably. 'I don't need to be mothered; I will *not* be mothered. And certainly I shouldn't have to remind you that these affairs in Sydney must be handled in person—by you—and handled properly.'

'Oh, pooh! I could do it just as well by telephone,' was the reply, but the tone of voice suggested an imminent compliance; Valerie was arguing for the sake of argument, and even Rena, judging by voice alone, could tell that.

Her arguments, Rena wasn't overjoyed to realise, fairly well paralleled Rena's own of the night before, although they went into detail she hadn't so much as considered. But finally Valerie Dunn appeared to agree. Then came the big surprise.

'Of course we still have to ascertain if Miss Everett will agree to this,' the woman said. 'And why you insist on inviting her to dinner tonight to broach the subject, I can't imagine. What are we going to talk about, for goodness' sake? She is, after all, hardly more than a child, Randall. And I daresay a fairly unsophisticated one, at that, living in this place.'

'Good,' snapped Ran, for the first time revealing how close he had come to the raw edge of his temper. 'Then if we stick to very small, two-syllable words, maybe it won't be too hard for her to realise that her only place in this is to keep a weather eye on things and not go interfering in my life. Now are you going up to issue the invitation, or shall I?'

'I shall,' said Valerie, and Rena could *see* the woman shaking her auburn head in displeasure. 'What's more, I'll do it now; I heard some noise a while ago, so she must be up already. Probably used to getting up early to feed chickens, or slop hogs or something.'

Rena didn't hear the reply in her frenzied scurry to get an elastic band round her hair in an impromptu ponytail and fling on the first clothes that came to hand—those she had been wearing the night before.

She barely had herself physically organised before the expected knock on her door, but she was totally, completely organised in her head. She would, she had immediately decided, refuse the invitation. Gracefully, regretfully, even. But she would refuse.

Five minutes later it was over. She would be joining Ran and his secretary for dinner at seven-thirty that evening, and she still didn't know what demon had taken over her tongue, changing gracious refusal into gracious acceptance without so much as a faltering word.

'I must be mad! Stark, raving, irrevocably mad,' she told herself in the mirror as the dinner hour approached and she stood naked, staring at herself and quite incapable of deciding what to wear.

Not that it mattered, certainly. Ran couldn't see her and Valerie Dunn's opinion was of little importance in the long run. Rena had one dress which she knew would perfectly suit the older woman's pre-formed

opinion of her. It had been one of her quasi-costumes
when singing in Sydney, a sort of peasant dress in gay
gingham, with puffy sleeves and a broad, squared-off
neckline. In it, with her hair short as it had been then,
she had looked about sixteen. Given a ponytail of her
much longer hair today and she might gain one year,
but hardly more than two.

She looked at herself, then at the dress, then turned
to the dress she had worn on that first, unforgettable
dinner date with Ran. Coil up her hair and wear *that*
dress, and Valerie Dunn would choke on her own
words!

The thought gave her a savage satisfaction, but the
gingham dress won. Rena deliberately ignored the
voice inside her that applauded the choice as a major
deterrent to the other woman changing her mind about
leaving Ran alone.

'The last thing I want anyway is to be left alone
with him,' she lied to herself in the mirror. 'He's a
bastard. . . an unscrupulous bastard who uses people and
then discards them. He's done it to me once and he'll
do it again, once this damned writing course is over.'

For one brief instant she contemplated throwing off
the dress and simply flouting the invitation. She could
just get in the old car and drive away, she thought.
Who could really object? Certainly not Ran, and Valerie Dunn was unlikely to bother. But she couldn't, in
the end, and at seven-thirty precisely she knocked on
the door of the flat below and presented herself like a
lamb to the slaughter.

The evening was, she decided later, undeniably,
unforgettably, unbelievably farcical! Like something
from a bad comedy. Black comedy.

Ran—wonder of wonders—had cooked the dinner,
and he made much of his comical efforts to peel
potatoes, slice young green beans and season the small

leg of lamb that was the main course. Almost, Rena decided, as if he was trying to prove something. His independence? While his recounting of the effort proved to be delightful comedy, it was not helped any by a continuous round of sniping from Valerie Dunn, who played hostess with an ill-disguised lack of enthusiasm.

It came as no surprise that Ran pretended this was his first-ever meeting with Rena, a charade both of them managed rather well, she thought later.

No mention was made of the writing classes, except in passing, derogatory terms by Valerie, nor of Ran's proposal that Rena should act as his Wednesday evening chauffeur. He quite deliberately kept the dinner conversation to broad general topics, ignoring Valerie's condescending attitude which came so close to outright rudeness that Rena had to bite her tongue on more than one occasion.

And when the subject of Rena 'looking out for me' came up, Ran chose to pass it off almost as an incidental afterthought. Valerie Dunn was much less casual, but nowhere near as difficult about the whole thing as Rena might have expected.

In Rena's eyes, the entire evening had an aura of fantasy about it. She and Ran seemed co-conspirators in a ludicrous, senseless black comedy. It was like a mingling of nightmares from which she felt certain to awake in another time, another place.

Not until she returned, quite early, to her own flat did Rena gradually begin to realise the skill with which Ran had manipulated the entire evening. More than the evening, the entire exercise of shifting Valerie Dunn out of his immediate future and Rena—despite her better judgment—into it.

Rena drifted into sleep that night wondering if she should not have listened to her better judgment. There

was something involved in all this that she didn't quite
understand, and the fact that Ran Logan certainly *did*
understand didn't help her one little bit.

She left for work early on Monday morning, thus
sparing herself the dubious pleasure of witnessing
Valerie's departure for the airport and the morning
flight south. And she didn't bother to go home for
dinner, but treated herself to a counter tea at the pub
before embarking upon her evening's work as an
entertainer.

It was one of her best nights ever. The audience, in
general, was young, enthusiastic, and most of all—
loudly appreciative. She had no time to worry about
returning to a house empty but for herself and Ran
Logan, no time to wonder if she had allowed herself to
be manipulated into something too dangerous for her
own good.

She sang a lot of her own compositions during the
evening, interspersing them with favourites like
'Greensleeves', 'Kilgary Mountain' and the various
Roger Whittaker songs she both loved and sang very
well. Much of the time the audience sang with her, but
even silent they went through a 'power of grog' in the
words of her overjoyed publican employer.

She joined him and his pleasant wife for drinks just
before closing, almost regretfully turning down his
invitation to double her engagements to two nights
each week.

'It's just not possible right now,' she replied, but
promised herself that one day . . . when Ran had finally
gone . . . then refused to let herself think of that day.
It would come all too soon as it was.

It was less easy not to think about Ran during the
long drive home, a drive during which she couldn't
help but wonder if he would be waiting up, expecting
to talk to her.

He wasn't, and she went to bed unsure if she was relieved or disappointed, lying in the pale moonlight with her ears knowingly alert to every nuance of sound in the flat below.

On Tuesday she didn't see him at all, which quite surprised her. Almost, indeed, to the point where she seriously debated the wisdom of going down to check on him when she returned home from work. But she didn't . . . and went to bed that night wondering whether she had done the right thing.

Rena spent a troubled night, part of her mind congratulating herself for being strong, for not allowing herself to fall for yet another Ran Logan ploy. Another part, however, worried. What if he'd fallen? What if he'd wandered off and got lost? What if . . .?

She needn't have worried; he was standing, a tall, lithe figure in faded blue jeans and a light T-shirt, waiting when she descended to her car the next morning.

'Any special place you'd like to have dinner tonight?' he asked without so much as a 'good morning' or 'how are you?' Then he grinned, a most engaging, little-boy grin. 'Or have you decided creative writing isn't your thing after all?' he asked.

Rena chose to ignore the disarming grin. 'I've decided you seem to be taking a great deal for granted,' she replied in her coolest voice. 'Perhaps it wasn't such a good idea to send your secretary away as you did.'

'Meeeow!' he retorted with a wider grin. 'I'll bet you're even more beautiful when you're touched by the old green-eyed monster.'

Rena gasped at the audacity of it, but before she could speak he was in ahead of her.

'Aw, go ahead and deny it,' he jibed. 'I'm sure both Louise and Valerie would be heartened, truly heartened, to know you're not in the least bit jealous.'

'You conceited . . . egotistical . . .' Rena couldn't go on. Her tongue was twisted into a knot that defied untangling. Her temper was creating a furnace inside her, but what could she do?

Ran blithely ignored her. 'How about we eat Chinese?' he asked as if it were the most logical question in the world. 'I manage quite well with chopsticks for a bloke who can't see what he's doing.'

'I think you've got your nerve!' she snapped, and then parroted his last remark in a high falsetto, before adding, 'How about we eat Australian, so I can watch you drooling pie and sauce all down the front of your stuffed shirt?'

'Oooh, aren't we bitter?' he retorted. 'Your trouble, Rena, is that you've got no sense of humour. It's all doom . . . doom . . . doom, with you.'

'And who wouldn't cry doom?' she snapped, all patience lost, 'being stuck with an egotistical, womanising cripple!'

'Now you're getting personal,' he replied without a hint of being upset by her remark. 'At least you could try fighting clean, although I suppose it's too much to expect from a confirmed manhater.'

'Clean? You wouldn't know the meaning of the word!' she snarled. All the worry and frustration of the past few days boiled to the surface in a flood of undiluted rage. 'You're nothing but a deceitful swine, Ran Logan, and I . . . I . . . hate you!'

'Okay,' he replied calmly, his tone of voice and attitude clearly designed to make her more angry still. 'But that still doesn't solve the problem about what we're having for dinner tonight.' He was so calm, so agreeable, so damned, deliberately *agreeable*.

'Well, as far as I'm concerned you can starve to death,' she cried. 'And if you're depending on me to make sure you're fed, you very well might just!'

'I am long past the stage of depending on a mere woman to ensure I'm fed,' he retorted. 'But not past the stage of inviting my chauffeur to join in my humble repast. So it'll be Chinese, then. What time shall I expect you?'

'You're impossible!'

'No,' he replied with maddening calm, 'just a wee bit improbable. Shall we say five-thirty? Or would six suit you better?'

'Shall we say ... never?' she retorted, voice alive with an anger she couldn't release because he wouldn't let her, wouldn't help her.

'No, my poor old stomach wouldn't stomach that,' he replied with a mocking grin. 'Don't be hard to get along with, Rena. You know—and I know—and you know that I know, et cetera, et cetera, et cetera, that you're going to give in in the end, so why not try and be gracious for a change?'

'Gracious? I'll give you *gracious*!' she snapped. 'Right where it'll do you the most good. And sideways, to boot!'

'Temper ... temper,' he cautioned. 'What are you so upset about, anyway? The fact that I started to make love to you the other night and you enjoyed it, or the fact that my damned blind clumsiness caused us to be interrupted so you didn't enjoy it enough?'

'Maybe it was just the fact you did it so badly,' she snarled. 'Not that I'd expect *that* to occur to you, since you obviously think you're the greatest thing since sliced bread.'

'Well, I certainly enjoyed it, up until the moment we were interrupted,' he replied. Quietly, calmly, without any evidence of temper. Infuriating, hateful man!

'I'm glad to see you make no attempt to defend yourself ... *and* your inadequacies,' Rena cried. 'Now if you don't mind I've got to leave for work.'

'And if I do mind?' There was a change in his voice
now; it was still resonant, but alive with a tension she
hadn't noticed before.

'I don't care whether you mind or not,' she shrieked.
'I think you're positively hateful!'

'And I,' he said in tones so calm, so deliberate that
she could have screamed, 'think you're beautiful.'

'And how the hell would you know?' She injected
the retort with every ounce of sarcasm she could
muster, ignoring the screams of protest from her
conscience. How brave, her conscience protested, to
bait a blind man. How noble, how childish, how . . .
wrong!

And how fruitless. Ran merely shrugged. 'I asked
John; I reckon he's a pretty fair judge of women.'

'You *what*?' Rena couldn't believe her ears. Nor
could she accept that Ran Logan would, blindly, accept
someone else's verdict on such a subject.

'Hah! I thought that'd surprise you,' he chuckled.
'But it's true. I asked him last Wednesday, when you
so conveniently *forgot* to come to class. He gives you
top marks, by the way, and from his description I can
understand why.'

'That's despicable!'

'I don't think so.' Again that careless, casual shrug.
Typical of Ran Logan; he could care less what anybody
else thought.

'And I don't care what you think!' temper, still boil-
ing, lent venom to her words.

'Oh, don't be silly, of course you do,' he replied.
'Otherwise you wouldn't have agreed to chauffeur me
. . . and to have dinner with me.'

'I've done no such thing. You suggested it and now
you seem to have blithely assumed I'd agreed. But *I*
have promised nothing whatsoever.' It sounded

smarmy even in her own ears; she wasn't surprised to see Ran's grin disappear.

'Ah,' he said. 'Perhaps you're right. Which means I've been guilty of a grievous sin, that of taking a lady for granted. And I do honestly apologise.' He made a slow, deliberate bow. 'Please, Miss Everett, would you take pity on a poor blind chap and offer him a lift to and from tonight's writing class?'

'Yes.' It wasn't a gracious reply, but Rena felt herself so totally trapped she couldn't be bothered being gracious. Damn the man anyway! He had her in a bind and he was obviously taking full advantage.

'And please, Miss Everett, will you accept my humble invitation to join me for dinner before we attend this class?' His voice was deliberately wheedling, deliberately calculated to annoy her. But behind those infernal reflective glasses she knew his eyes were laughing, blind or not.

'Only if you promise to lay off the blind beggar act,' she snapped. 'It doesn't become you at all.'

'All right!' he snapped, suddenly angry. 'And in return you might try to stop blaming me for what somebody else did to you. I have been a proper bastard once or twice in my time and I probably will be again, but at the moment I'm sick and tired of copping the flak for somebody else's nastiness!'

Rena couldn't reply; she was dumbstruck by the anger in him, by the sheer enormity of his rage.

He began speaking again, this time in a voice so soft, so threateningly low, that she had to strain to hear him. 'I don't deny you've probably got a right to be bitter,' he hissed. 'And if you want to spend the rest of your life as a manhater that's your business. But leave me out of it, because whatever else I'd done, in this particular case I am *not* to blame!'

'Oh yes, you are!' Anger spewed out the statement

before Rena could stop herself, and once it was said
she could only stand there, mouth open and eyes wide
with shock. She was at least as surprised by the words
as Ran himself.

He had started to turn away, but her words froze
him in place like a gaunt statue. It seemed hours before
he turned back to face her.

'And just what the hell is *that* supposed to mean?'
His voice was still soft, but beneath the velvet was cold,
rigid steel, the chill of an Arctic ice pack.

'I . . . I . . .' She couldn't get it out. Could not, *dared*
not. Forget the anger, forget the hatred she had
deliberately cultivated during the past two years. Here
was Ran Logan, here before her as she had so often
dreamed, but she couldn't throw her gauntlet of betrayal into the face of a blind man.

But she must say something. Only what? Her mind
churned uselessly, revolving round words but unable
to grasp even *one* that could provide salvation. And
Ran was waiting with the patience of a wild beast.

Rena's hands clenched and unclenched, her nails
digging mine-shafts in her palms. Ran's fists were also
clenched, but they were as rigid as the rest of his pos-
ture, alive with anger, unmoving because of his iron
control.

'Well?' The single word emerged from lips taut with
anger, but he didn't give her any chance to reply. 'Oh,
forget it,' he sneered. 'Forget everything! I'd a thousand times rather be blind my way than yours; at least
there's the vague hope that I'll recover. So keep your
manhating ways, Rena, and bloody well be welcome to
them!'

She was still standing, open-mouthed and speech-
less, as he turned on his heel and strode away. He had
to fumble with outstretched hands to find the doorway
into his flat, but once that was done he had no difficulty

opening the door—and then slamming it behind him so loudly that the entire building seemed to shake.

Rena, too, was shaking, trembling so badly she had to reach out and lean on her car for support. Her knees felt like spaghetti and the turmoil inside made her fear for an instant she was going to be sick.

When, finally, she got into the vehicle and drove slowly into the city to work, she found the highlights of their unbelievable conversation running over and over in her mind, like an endless, meaningless tape. Throughout the day she mulled it over, trying desperately to justify her own part in the scene, but it wasn't easy.

'But how can I justify being a bitch?' she asked herself aloud on the way home, having left work a few minutes early so as to be sure and catch Ran before he left—if he left—for dinner without her. She would apologise; she must. And it wouldn't, she realised, be easy.

Nor was it, not least because it seemed to take a lifetime before he answered her knock at the door. And when he did, the face that confronted her was bleak, expressionless.

'I've come to apologise for this morning,' Rena blurted before she could lose her nerve entirely.

'All right.' The mirrored sunglasses hid too much of his face, but what could be seen held little promise of any real acceptance.

'And ... and if your dinner invitation is still open, I'd ... like very much to come with you,' she said, forcing out the words, angry now with herself and Ran as well. Damn him! He was as wrong as she, had been even more provocative ... why did *he* not apologise?

'Shall we say half an hour, then?' he said instead. 'I'll need that long to get changed, and I'm sure you'll want to freshen up after a day in the office.'

'Half an hour will be fine,' Rena agreed with a sigh. 'I'll see you then.'

When she knocked on the door the second time, having changed into a light, casual dress, Ran was waiting for her and opened up without delay. But he said little until they were in the car and heading for town.

'I suppose you're waiting for me to apologise as well,' he said then. 'I probably should, since I imagine I had a hand in making you lose your temper, but I'm not going to, Rena.'

'Nobody said you have to,' she replied, her voice as cool as his. This was stupid, she thought. She'd apologised, he wouldn't, and they were no better off than before except that he'd got his own way in the end.

'You're going to have to get over this business of being a manhater,' he said, quite ignoring her remark. 'You're a young woman with your whole life ahead, and that kind of blind bitterness is only destructive. Believe me, I know.'

'Are you so good at taking your own advice, then?' she asked hotly. 'I've certainly got the impression you're doing your best to take out your own bitterness on whatever woman happens to be handy.'

'You think that because I kissed you, started to make love to you, I was merely using you? Lord, I knew you were bitter, but I hadn't realised you were totally naïve as well.'

'I'm not.'

'Well then, stop talking as if you are. I kissed you because I wanted to, and I'd have made love to you because we both wanted it. But I wasn't using you to take out either my bitterness or any other frustrations you might imagine.'

'Of course not,' she sneered. 'You've got plenty of women willing to help solve your frustrations, haven't you?'

'An infinite number,' he replied—and then, surprisingly, grinned. 'So let's change the subject before we get the war going all over again. How's your writing going?'

'It isn't; probably because arguing with you all the time has put me right off,' she replied. And then, realising he couldn't see that she was joking, she hastily added, 'I shall very likely have to bring you an apple to class tonight, or you'll have me doing extra homework or something.'

'Just be happy they've outlawed the cane, that's all I have to say,' Ran replied with a chuckle. 'Although the way this class is going, you might have to stand in line.'

'You mean I'm not the worst? And here I've been trying so hard, too.' Lightness in her voice; she would keep up this façade of bantering friendliness, Rena thought. It was better than fighting.

'Hardly. You, at least, seem to be taking the thing relatively seriously, which is more than I can say for one or two others.'

'But you're not going to tell me who, are you?' she teased. 'Professional ethics and all that.'

'Not a bit of it. And you'll be able to see for yourself without being told, I have no doubt of that.'

They arrived at the restaurant then, and the topic of discussion changed to food, a much less controversial subject and one where Rena felt considerably more comfortable.

They dined on a variety of Oriental offerings, which Ran dealt with as skilfully as he had promised. During the meal they talked about many things, but none were personal or terribly controversial, and by the time they finally reached the college it seemed Ran's mood was much improved.

He handled the class in a singularly jovial fashion,

mingling praise with criticism and seemingly quite unaffected by the fact that hardly anybody seemed to have done much writing since the week before.

Old John greeted Rena with a warm smile of welcome and a knowing wink, Louise with a scowl and a series of petulant glances that made *her* opinion of Rena's return to class abundantly obvious.

The redhead seemed bent on monopolising Ran as much as she possibly could, while Ran himself seemed equally bent on frustrating her. He was never rude, never even so pointed in his remarks as to upset her, but he was keeping his distance, even if Louise couldn't—or wouldn't—take the hint.

She immediately cornered him once the formal class was over, and Rena, not wanting to interrupt, had moved to the opposite corner of the room when John approached with a broad grin and blew her world apart in a single comment.

'Just wanted to say how much I enjoyed your singing the other night, Rena.' The words boomed like thunder in the small room as he promised to come and listen again the following Monday.

CHAPTER SEVEN

RENA felt the blood drain from her suddenly light head, saw the room dissolve into a kaleidoscope of flickering lights as a wave of some strange tingling sensation enveloped her body.

She didn't hear John's next words, but she felt his hands as he gripped her upper arms and slowed her descent, guiding her so that she landed in the nearest seat.

'Put your head between your knees,' he ordered, hands still supporting her as she obeyed. And then did he whisper, 'I'm sorry?' Rena thought so, but his voice was crowned in the surf of the blood flowing back to her bewildered brain.

Altogether, the performance couldn't have lasted a minute, but it was the longest single minute in Rena's life. She simply couldn't believe her eyes when she looked around, finally, to see that Ran and Louise were only just starting to move across the room towards her.

'Oh, what happened?' cried Louise, the look on her face belying any real concern.

'Just a dizzy spell,' John replied with an amazingly calm voice and a steady glance to help cover up his lie.

'Yes, it's all right now,' Rena added in a lie of her own. 'I think perhaps I must have over-eaten at dinner or something.'

Ran said nothing and the face behind the sunglasses was impassive. But he knew! He'd heard! He *must* have.

And yet when he did speak, after what seemed an awfully long time to Rena, his voice betrayed no hint that her secret was out, that he couldn't possibly now ignore that one coincidence too many between the girl he had known in Sydney and the one who now played chauffeur under a different name.

'You're sure that's all it is, Rena?' he asked. And he *sounded* genuinely concerned. So genuinely concerned that Louise, an expert herself in attention-getting manoeuvres, shot Rena a look of pure malevolence.

'I'm fine, really I am. Now why don't you two go back to whatever you were discussing? I'm just going to sit a moment and then perhaps I'll join you,' Rena said.

Louise needed no encouragement. Tugging possessively at Ran's arm, she steered him back to the far corner of the room, her lips close to his ear as she whispered something neither Rena nor John could hear.

'You *are* all right, I hope?' John asked quietly.

'For the moment,' she replied with a rueful attempt at a grin. 'I'm really sorry to have . . . fainted, but you gave me a terrible shock.'

'And from such an innocuous comment, too,' he grinned. 'I don't know what game you're playing, young Rena, but I really do think you're out of your depth. And I warned you about that, too, remember?'

'How could I forget? And it doesn't matter any more, I suspect. If it . . . if it ever did.'

'Humph! Of course it does,' he retorted. 'Your problem is that you have too little faith. Anyhow, sorry if I queered your pitch. I shall have to try keeping my big mouth firmly shut from now on.'

Rena wanted to reassure him; he looked even more concerned about the whole thing than she was herself. But before she could reply, her glance caught Ran and Louise approaching once again, so she had to content herself with only a forgiving smile for dear John.

'I think it's time we were off, Rena, if you feel fit enough to make the journey,' Ran said without preamble. 'And if you don't, for goodness' sake say so. We can always arrange a cab or something.'

He should never know, she thought, how much that idea appealed. The presence of another person would have to at least delay the confrontation she knew would begin as soon as they were alone together in her car. But . . . what sense?

'I'm fine, honestly,' she replied. 'Unless, of course, you feel unsafe about riding back with me. A woman driver is one thing, but one who has dizzy spells . . .'

The attempt at humour was wasted. Even John

didn't smile. And a few minutes later Rena was where she least wanted to be, behind the wheel of her car, with Ran. Alone!

Now, she told herself. Surely he'll hit me with it now, not wait until we're out in the traffic. Not after knowing how shaken up I was.

But he didn't. And if Rena was a trembling bundle of anticipatory nerves during the drive home, Ran was, if anything, the complete opposite—implacable, quiet, withdrawn. Not, she was surprised to notice, angry or sullen or intense, as she might have expected. Merely remote, as if he were lost in a thought world of his own.

When they arrived back at the house, he emerged only long enough to thank her for her company at dinner, her effort in providing transportation, and to bid her a courteous but definite goodnight.

'I hope you don't suffer any more problems with dizziness,' he concluded. 'Not that I'd be much help, but if you do have a problem just thump on the floor or something.'

It was his only even remotely personal comment since dinner, and hardly sufficient to soothe Rena's throbbing, over-excited nerves.

She climbed the stairs to her own flat in a total quandary. Had he missed John's remark? It didn't seem possible, but surely he must have. Not even Ran Logan could have failed to put two and two together after hearing such a comment.

She lay down, but couldn't sleep. Guilt was a tangible presence in her bedroom, and the fact that she could find no resolution to her guilt didn't help at all.

At one stage she even considered going down and having it out with Ran, confessing everything. But she didn't, and knew deep inside that she wouldn't. Not while he was blind.

She rose next morning, puffy-eyed from lack of sleep and with her head feeling as if it was stuffed with cotton wool. Her descent to the carport when it came time to go to work was tentative, cautious. But in vain. Ran wasn't waiting to confront her with her duplicity; nor was he waiting when she got home that evening.

Rena didn't see him on Friday, either, except as a shadowy figure that was barely visible when she peered in the lounge room window, now becoming somewhat concerned for him, instead of herself.

But on Saturday he appeared, so early that when he knocked on her door she had to call out to him to wait and scurry into the first clothes she could find. It wasn't until she had answered the door to find him waiting with a vaguely impatient scowl on his face that she realised her hurried dressing hadn't really been necessary.

'I'm sorry, I didn't mean to wake you,' he said, and on being assured that she was awake, merely not quite presentable, he grinned.

'That's the worst thing about being blind; you miss out on almost all the fun,' he said. 'But that wasn't what I came for. Are you doing anything tomorrow?'

Was she? Of course she wasn't, but caution made her hesitate. Was Ran setting her up for something? Had he somehow managed to hold back his confrontation until he could arrange an appropriate time, an appropriate setting?

'Please don't let me upset anything you've already planned,' he said then, obviously sensing her hesitation.

'No ... no,' she hastened to assure him. 'There's nothing planned that's important enough to worry about.' Actually, she had nothing planned at all, but she dared not admit it.

'I'd like to ask quite a large favour,' he said. 'Is there

a nice beach somewhere near ... some place we might go for a long walk and have a talk?'

Rena drew a deep breath. Was this it, then? And yet, somehow, she felt that it wasn't. Not even Ran was so consummate an actor as this.

'I imagine I could find somewhere,' she replied. 'But if you want to talk about something, why not here ... now?' And at least, she thought we can get it over with if it's a confrontation he wants. But no such luck.

'I need the exercise, among other things,' he grinned. 'And I've still got a bit of thinking to do before ... well, before I ask your opinion about what I have in mind.'

'I suppose you realise it's cruel to prey upon my curiosity,' Rena said then, her brows furrowed as she tried with her usual lack of success to read his expression.

'But of course; that's the whole idea,' he replied, then flatly refused to provide so much as a hint about what he wanted to discuss. Instead he nodded politely in acceptance of a ten o'clock start, and turned away to make his cautious journey back down the staircase.

Ran was waiting for her when Rena emerged next morning after another typically tortured night with little sleep and far too much thinking. He stood at the bottom of her staircase, leaning casually against the balustrade, clad in only a pair of cut-off blue jean shorts and a faded, matching shirt that was open practically to the waist.

He *looked* up at her approach, briefly, then lowered his head against as if in realisation that he might look but never see. As she reached the bottom of the stairs, Rena's own eyes were caught by the glint of his medallion—her medallion—in the bright sunlight.

She couldn't see Ran's eyes behind his reflective glasses, but was relieved to see that he was smiling when she reached the bottom of the stairs.

'We should have started this much earlier,' he said. 'It's going to be hot as hell.'

'Well all you had to do was ask,' she retorted. 'I've been up practically since dawn, and I imagine you have as well.'

'No such luck; I don't suffer from too much light interrupting my sleep, don't forget,' he replied. But not angrily, not grimly, not even really bitterly.

'Anyway, am I suitably dressed for the occasion? I thought if you don't mind playing seeing-eye dog I'd forget my damned white stick today and try to look halfways normal at least.'

'You look marvellous,' Rena replied. And it was no lie; her heart fairly leapt at the sight of his lean, muscular body, a body she had once known so intimately. As he had known hers. She was dressed just as casually as Ran, although her own shirt wasn't open quite to the waist and she had her bikini on underneath it and her faded board shorts.

'No compliments, please. You'll turn my head and make me even more conceited than you already think I am,' he replied with a wide grin. Rena returned it, but she couldn't help wondering what had happened to put him in such a cheerful frame of mind.

He was generally quiet during their long drive to Moore Park, a small beach settlement about twenty miles north of Bundaberg. To get there meant considerable back-tracking, since they had to drive all the way into the city so as to cross the Burnett River before working their way back towards the coast, but Ran had said he wanted a long walk, and Rena was determined to give it to him.

From the kiosk at Moore Park there was nothing but a straight line of beach for miles to the north. If he wished, they could walk all the way to where the Kolan

River merged with the sea at Miara.

She parked her vehicle beneath a huge, spreading she-oak on the edge of the dunes, and a few moments later they were carefully negotiating the track down to the hard-packed sand of the beach.

It was a tricky exercise, hampered both by the deep, soft sand and the fact that Ran seemed determined to manage with as little help as possible. It wasn't until he slipped and fell for the second time that he ungraciously accepted Rena's hand.

'Damned nuisance,' he muttered. 'Sorry, Rena . . . not you. I should have brought the bloody stick, I guess. I'd forgotten how difficult it is to walk in soft sand, even when you can see where you're going.'

'I think you've done wonderfully,' she replied, gasping just a little at the effort of trying to maintain both his balance and her own. For the first time, she realised how much wiser it might have been to enter the beach from the main parking area, where the track was better.

But by then they had reached the hard-packed sand left by the ebbing tide; Rena had actually timed things quite well and the damp sand made a good footpath.

'Ah, this is better,' said Ran, turning unerringly towards the sea and throwing back his head to let the brisk sea-breeze ruffle his hair. 'Point me towards the water and stop me before I get to New Zealand,' he said. 'It feels like forever since I had a swim.'

'But . . . but . . . should you?' she asked. Was he crazy, hellbent on some ridiculous suicide mission? Her own uncertainty was tinged by real fear.

'You're damned right I should,' he replied with a grim chuckle. 'Not only *should*; I'm going to. You can stay here and guard my sunglasses.'

'I will not! If you're mad enough to try swimming when you can't even see what you're doing, then I'm

coming too,' Rena cried. 'But at least give me a minute
to strip down to my swimsuit.'

'I'd even help you,' he said with a wicked grin, 'but
I know that's not on, so I'll just go on ahead and you
can catch up at your own pace.'

And to Rena's astonishment, he placed his sunglasses into the hand he had been holding, then
plunged straight for the sea at a steady, determined
trot. He slowed when the water splashed against his
bare ankles, slowed even more when it reached to his
muscular thighs. But he didn't stop, and seemed oblivious to the fact that his clothing was being soaked.

'Ran!' She screamed his name out twice, but he
didn't listen . . . or didn't appear to. Rena flung off her
clothing with careless haste and plunged after him,
unsure of his true intentions.

But when she finally reached him, in water so deep
she nearly had to swim to where he stood spraddle-
legged against the power of the waves, he laughed a
huge, joyful greeting as her hand closed on his arm.

'Isn't it terrific? Fantastic!' And he flung himself
backwards with the next wave to emerge dripping but
still laughing as he scrabbled for his balance.

Rena flung herself almost as quickly, afraid he might
become disorientated under water, but by the time she
reached his side again he was in total control, giving
himself to the surging power of the waves, riding the
water and quite oblivious to any dangers.

Even when a wave, unseen, smashed across his face
and left him spluttering for breath, he merely shook
himself free and lurched towards the shallower water
close to shore.

'You're mad!' Rena finally caught up, her anger
tinged with disbelief at the carelessness of his attitude.
'What are you trying to do—kill yourself?'

'Of course not. I'm just having fun,' he replied,

shouting against the noise of rushing sea and brisk wind. Even as he finished speaking, a breaking wave thrust him off balance, throwing him against Rena so that they fell together in the waist-deep water.

She felt his arms close around her, reached out to grip him with her own, unable to ignore the flow of desire that raced through her at the feel of his bare legs against her own, his muscular chest grinding against her breasts. But when they struggled to their feet, Ran released her quickly, almost as if the touch of her was repugnant to him.

'Maybe you're right,' he muttered. 'We'd better start on our walk before I do something dangerously stupid.' Letting the waves guide him, he ploughed ashore, then stood waiting as Rena fetched her clothing and his sunglasses.

As she did so, her mind replayed his last words, words so ambiguous she had to wonder what he had meant. Dangerously stupid—to play in the sea? she wondered. Or to hold her in his arms as he had? She decided either answer would be too correct.

Ran's mood seemed to have been drastically altered by his return to land. As they strolled slowly along the tide mark, he remained silent, demanding by his very attitude that Rena do likewise. Nor did he require much help from her; instead of holding her hand, as she had rather expected, he strode confidently beside her, using the feel of the wetness at his feet, the wind, and the sound of the sea beside him for guides.

The beach was firm and flat as far as the eye could see. Nothing on which to stumble, nothing to hamper his movements. Only on the rare occasions when his balance fooled him did he reach out to her for stability.

The sun was warm, but not unbearably so. Just enough, indeed, to dry them quickly and keep them comfortable. It wasn't the time of year for swimming and the water had been cold, though Rena hadn't noticed that because of her concern and Ran simply didn't appear to have noticed.

They walked ... and walked ... and walked. Silently, almost like two strangers sharing a path. But there was a tension; Rena could feel it tangibly building between them. Still, when Ran finally broke the silence, it was so unexpected it startled her.

'I need your advice.' It was strangely said, the words flat and harsh, defensive.

'What about?' Her own reply was equally flat, but merely cautious.

'A problem.'

'Well, I rather assumed that,' she replied gently. 'But I will need a bit more information if I'm to advise you.'

He didn't answer for a moment, walking half a dozen, a dozen steps first. Then he stopped abruptly and turned to face her.

'You remember I mentioned a ... woman who disappeared rather abruptly when she found out I was blind?'

'Of course.'

'Well, I think I know now where she is.' The remark struck at Rena like a slap in the face. He *still* loved this woman, she thought with amazement. How could he? A woman who had abandoned him at a time when he needed her most, and he still loved her.

'I ... I'm not sure what you want me to say,' Rena faltered.

'I had thought I might go to her, face her with it, see what she says.' It sounded like a decision, but his voice told a different tale; he was asking if he should do these things, not announcing a firm decision.

'What do you think it would accomplish?' Rena was

floundering because she didn't know what else to say, what possible advice she might provide that would make sense.

He shrugged, shaking his head to let the wind ruffle his hair. 'I might get some answers, that's all.'

'You're . . . still very much in love with her, aren't you?' Rena didn't have to ask, she knew. Worse, she knew just how easy it could be, because she was still in love with Ran, and now realised she always had been. Despite his deceptions, despite his abandonment of her, despite his blindness . . . especially that.

'I suppose that sounds quite ridiculous to you,' he said grimly. 'It should; *I* think it's ridiculous. Only I can't seem to do much about it.'

'No,' she replied very softly, forcibly halting herself from reaching out to him, from taking his hand. 'No, I don't think it's ridiculous.'

'Well, you should.' And for the first time she felt the barb of bitterness in his voice. 'You're obviously not still in love with the chap that did the dirty on you. Or are you?'

Of course I am, she thought, but she said nothing. What could she say? A lie to make him wonder even more at his own logic, or the truth, the truth that had become disguised and abused and twisted out of reason by her own deceptions?

'Humph! Better no answer than a lie to make me feel good,' he grunted. And something inside Rena cried out at the horrible tangle of duplicity she had woven. Ran needed the truth from her; it might be all she could ever provide for her love, but she dared not.

'Mind you, it may not come to anything anyway,' he said, apparently forgetting his earlier question. 'I'm . . . still not a hundred per cent sure that she's . . . where I think.' And then, explosively, 'But I'll find out, damn it! I've got to.' And he laughed, the bitter, mocking laugh of a man condemned without hope. 'Not that it's going to matter a damn; she'll likely just keep on lying to me, as she's always done.'

Rena shuddered at the violence so close to the surface. 'If you feel that way, I wonder if it would be wise to see her,' she said. 'I mean . . . well . . .'

'I know what you mean,' he growled. 'But you forget—if I can just catch her in a lie, I might give myself the purely personal satisfaction of breaking her lovely neck. That might be the way to solve all my problems at once.'

'Oh, stop it!' Rena snapped. 'That's no way to be thinking and you know it.' His sincerity frightened her, it wasn't angry enough to be passed over. He *meant* it!

He sneered. 'For a manhater you preach a pretty soft line,' he countered. 'Are you going to tell me you wouldn't like to do something similar to *your* ex-lover if you had the chance? Well, don't, because I wouldn't believe you.'

'There . . . was a time when I wanted to, yes,' she agreed. Why argue with him? It was truthful enough to admit it.

'But no longer? What's the matter, Rena—going soft in your old age?' It was a sneering, almost vicious attack, clearly geared to make her angry.

'There's no sense goading me,' she replied as calmly as she could manage. 'You invited me to advise you, not stand about giving you something to vent your anger on.'

'You mean you won't fight with me.'

'I mean I don't want to fight with you. Save your fighting for when you locate this woman,' she snapped. 'You once accused me—I might remind you—of taking out my manhating on you . . . perhaps you should heed your own advice.'

'Advice is usually only worth what you pay for it,'

he snorted. 'Which makes mine, particularly, pretty damned useless.'

'Oh,' Rena replied hotly, more hotly than she really intended. 'Does that mean I'm to be paid for today? Or just that having asked my advice you're intending to ignore it?'

'Ah! Who knows?' he retorted angrily. 'I'm not certain *I* do any more, that's a fact. For two . . . too long now I've thought that if I could find the bitch I'd wring her neck for her, and now that I'm close to it, I'm not sure it would be worth the trouble.'

'Revenge is a destructive emotion, especially to the person seeking revenge,' said Rena, then shuddered at how patronising it sounded, how pompous. And yet true. She no longer felt vengeful about Ran Logan, although she was sick of herself for establishing such a tangle of lies and deceit around their whole situation since he had come to Bundaberg.

No, revenge was not the answer. At least not for her. Indeed there *was* no answer. Nothing now could save her from eventually having to admit her real identity to Ran, but without explaining the reasons for her deception. That she could never do . . . how to explain her love for him, her feeling of betrayal, when his own experience was so vivid and so aggravated by his blindness?

Her only hope was that he would complete his teaching assignment and return to Sydney without ever discovering her identity. That would be best; it could mean nothing to him anyway. And yet surely there must be something, some feeling on his part. Else why seek her advice? Why seek her company?

'Betrayal is just as destructive—to the one who's on the receiving end,' he replied. 'You can't argue that one, can you, Rena?'

'No, I can't,' she admitted. 'But as you seem intent

on telling me, sometimes, you're young; your whole
life is ahead of you. Why fill it with bitterness? Why
not just forget the past and look ahead?'

'Look ahead? *Look* ahead?' His voice dropped so low
she could barely hear him, but the venom in his words
was coarse as the ocean spray. 'By God, but you've got
an interesting way with words. And tell me, darling
Rena, just what am I to look ahead *with*? What am I to
look ahead *to*?'

His eyes blazed when he flung off the sunglasses to
reveal them, but it was a lifeless fire, without direction
or focus.

Still, it was a relief to Rena when he finally replaced
the reflective glasses, hiding at least part of his bitter
anger behind their mirrors. The rest, however, lived in
his voice, in his every gesture.

'Look ahead . . .' he whispered. His hand went out
to fumble towards hers, and unthinking, she reached
out to him, put her fingers in the hardness of his grasp.
Then, without warning, she was in his arms, crushed
against him as his mouth sought her lips.

It was no kiss of pleasure, no kiss of friendliness,
not even of need. It was brutal, demanding, taking.
Her lips were parted beneath his searching mouth, her
neck strained backwards as he forced her head back,
his hands locked at her waist.

'Is this what I'm to look ahead to?' he demanded
when the fury of the kiss was over and his lips had left
her mouth sore and swollen. 'To kissing a woman I
can't see? To touching her, not knowing what she looks
like, whether she enjoys the touch or hates it? To never
knowing if any woman I touch is repulsed by me, is
lying to me, cheating me?'

He laughed, a bitter, brittle laugh of pure scorn. His
fingers unlocked from behind her, one hand shifting
round to close against her breast, fingers stroking,

caressing, rousing her nipple to firmness. Rena wanted to speak, to move, to do *something*. But she could only stand and endure his harsh caress.

'See? Your body reacts—I don't need eyes to know that. But do *you* react? Do you enjoy this . . .' and his fingers created heaven for her '. . . or do you simply endure, humouring the harmless lusts of a poor blind man?'

His arms closed around again, pulling her against him, forcing her to accept the hardness of his masculinity against her soft, pliant body. Then he thrust her from him in a gesture so abrupt and violent that she stumbled and almost fell.

Ran spun in a circle, arms outstretched like some gaunt sacrifice. 'Harmless, see?' he chided. 'While I hold you, there's something between us, but once free . . . you've nothing to fear from a man who can't see you. Not . . . one . . . damned . . . thing! Isn't that something for me to *look* forward to?'

Then he halted, arms suddenly listless at his side. The anger left his face, to be replaced by a bitterness Rena could almost taste.

'Great advice you offer,' he said. 'And if I took it? What would you think then, Rena, if I took your damned advice and *looked* ahead? Would you care? Would you be there for me to touch, give you something live to vent your own bitterness on? Hell, maybe that's a great idea. I'd be just right for you; you could hate me as much as you wanted to, take any advantage you liked . . . because I couldn't fight back.'

'Stop it! Oh, please . . . *stop it*! she cried. It was too painful; she couldn't listen. But he wouldn't stop.

'Why?' he shouted back at her, his voice like acid. 'Don't you think it would be a great arrangement? Think how nice it would be. You could betray me without me ever even knowing; you could give me dirty looks without having to go behind my back; you could make me totally, completely, uselessly dependent on you—and when you got sick of me you could just walk away, knowing that I couldn't see to stop you.'

'No!' She screamed it the first time, then repeated it over and over in an endless litany of shame and sorrow.

'No.' His own voice echoed her. 'No, perhaps you wouldn't, Rena. But *she* would; most women damned well would. And even if you didn't, eventually you'd get sick of being lumbered with half a man, an overgrown baby you have to take out on a leash.'

He paused, and when he continued it was in a voice so low that the rush of the waves nearly drowned it out. 'It's too bad you're not the manhater you pretend to be, Rena. I think it might have been a bloody good arrangement.'

She didn't reply. She couldn't, short of screaming her answer over her shoulder. Ran's final caustic words were too much for her. Eyes half blinded by her own tears, her own guilt, she fled, running up the beach and leaving him to stand alone, crying his bitter soliloquy to the seagulls and the wind.

CHAPTER EIGHT

SHE ran blindly, as blindly as Ran himself might have done it. But she didn't run far. Even in her pain, some small part of her mind refused to leave him standing there, a prisoner of his infirmity.

Soon—too soon for her—she returned. Walking, this time, her feet digging into the hard-packed sand and her breath heaving with her earlier exertions.

Ran knew she was there. She approached silently,

but he knew! He turned as she approached, searching with blind eyes, his other senses compensating.

'You might as well say it,' he growled. 'I'm a proper bastard and I admit it. What am I?'

'You're a proper bastard,' said Rena, honouring the remark in a listless voice. 'And I guess that makes two of us.'

'No, one is quite enough,' he said. 'Will you hold my hand on the way back? I'm beginning to think I've had too much sun or something; I don't feel real crash hot.'

They were a quarter of the way back to the car before Rena spoke again, and she did it hesitantly, unsure of her ground.

'You're going to finish it, aren't you?' she asked. 'If only to hear this . . . this woman put in her own words why she left you when you might have needed her the most.'

'I reckon. Sounds stupid, doesn't it? But I have to hear it from her own lips, if only to clear the devils from my mind.' His fingers squeezed Rena's lightly. 'And I *am* sorry for jumping on you so hard back there. I get so . . . just so damned frustrated, sometimes.'

'Forget it.' Her own guilt was enough to bear, without adding to it by harassing him further.

'All right. I'll make it up to you somewhere along the line anyway,' he said.

They strolled along in silence for quite some time before he spoke again. 'I'll say one thing for you, Rena . . . you may be a manhater, but at least I know where I stand with you. That sounds horribly patronising, doesn't it? But it isn't meant to be. I mean, *you* wouldn't be bothered feeding me a whole lot of bull-dust, would you? Easier just to be straight and let the chips fall where they may. I quite like that.'

He might have; Rena shuddered inside with every word. Her own guilt, a guilt that seemed to grow no matter how much she attempted to justify her deception of Ran, was beginning to twist itself into a permanent knot inside her.

'I don't think you should take me as any classic example,' she replied, trying to lighten the conversation. 'I'm just . . . well, perhaps a bit weird, when you come right down to it. In fact, I'm beginning to wonder a bit about me.'

'I wouldn't if I were you. You're a warm, caring person, despite your bitterness. One day you'll meet the right man and the past will just . . . disappear.'

How easy for him to say, Rena thought. But the past wouldn't disappear, not until Ran Logan himself disappeared. And when, she wondered, would that be? Obviously not until he had confronted his dream girl and sorted out his mind on that score, but if she . . . if *she* continued to torment him, would he ever abandon the dream for a reality? It wouldn't matter to her, Rena thought. She couldn't possibly recreate any form of personal relationship, not after the deceptions she had been weaving since he had turned up again in her world.

If she were to tell him, now, that she was Catherine Conley as well as Rena Everett, what might it do to him? Bad enough that one woman had shattered his illusions . . . for Rena to reveal her own deceptions would be adding insult to injury.

Despite the certain knowledge, in recent weeks, that he might *suspect*, that he couldn't fail to notice the similarities in voice, in attitude, in . . . *whatever*, Rena simply couldn't force herself to come clean, opening up her own situation to allow nothing but pain for them both.

'You don't really believe me, do you?' he asked, not

waiting for an answer. 'But it will, you know. One morning when you're older, when you've got your life together with just the right bloke, you'll wake up and find you can't even remember the swine who deserted you.'

'I don't think it's quite that simple,' she replied, 'but I hope you're right.' Only she knew he wasn't right. She would never be able to forget Ran Logan, now or later.

Fortunately, he let the conversation lapse there, and for the rest of their journey back to the car he was silent. Apart from the light, almost negligible touching of their hands, they might have been walking totally apart, each lost in their own thoughts.

Rena put it down to Ran having got, as he'd suggested, a bit too much sun. But by the time they reached the house again she realised it was worse than that—he'd got a *lot* too much sun. His complexion, rather fairer than her own, now blazed crimson across his face, his chest and arms and on the back of his neck. Even his legs showed a touch of burn.

And he wasn't well. Not that he wanted to admit it, but having been raised in Queensland, Rena knew all about the vivid dangers of the deceptive sub-tropical sunshine. When they reached home, Ran's forehead was beaded in sweat, his hair soaked with it.

She had to help him from the car, and it took no great comprehension to realise he was unsteady on his feet; Rena had some difficulty getting him inside his own flat and finally seated in the first handy chair.

'Oh, lord . . . I'm really sorry,' she said. 'This is my fault. How could I have been so stupid?'

'I found it rather easy,' he replied in a shaky voice. 'And it isn't your fault, so stop complaining. I'll be okay; I just need to rest a bit, that's all.'

He took several deep breaths, then swallowed convulsively. 'Only first I think I'm going to be sick.'

And he was, horribly sick. Rena only just managed to get him into the bathroom in time. When that was over, she embarked on a furious search for a thermometer, praying now that he was only suffering heat exhaustion and not a serious case of sunstroke.

'I'm all right,' he kept insisting, even trying to talk around the thermometer once she had located it and stuck it in his mouth.

'You're not all right,' she countered. 'Now shut up and let me take your temperature, or I'm going straight out to call for an ambulance. I may have to, anyway.'

She hoped not. His symptoms were more those of the less serious heat exhaustion—skin not hot and dry, but perspiring furiously; his temperature close to the century but not the hundred and five it might be in the case of heat-stroke.

But he must be cooled off, and reasonably quickly, if not by the severe methods recommended for heat-stroke. Rena didn't think about it too long.

'Get your clothes off,' she demanded, reaching at the same time to turn on the shower and adjust the spray so that the emerging water was cool but not at full coldness.

'I will not!' It was almost a shocked reaction, but she was in no mood to argue.

'You'll do as I say.' But he wasn't going to, she could tell. 'Well, at least take your shirt off, damn it. This is serious, Ran.'

When he still hesitated, Rena did not. She reached out and snatched at the front of the shirt, ripping downward so that buttons flew like missiles around the small room. Once the shirt was open, she yanked him around and back until she had it off, then steered him beneath the shower spray.

He shuddered at the impact of the water on his sunburned neck. He would have got out of it, but she screamed at him, pleaded with him, abused him and physically prevented him from doing what he wanted.

Oblivious to the soaking of her own clothing, she used her hands to sluice the cool water across his broad shoulders, cupping her fingers to hold it momentarily at the nape of his neck. Ran stood still, breathing deeply but saying nothing, until she was done.

'Now come out of there and get dried off,' she said, taking his hand and thrusting a towel into it as she turned off the shower. Suddenly nervous, she retreated to the bathroom door, calling back over her shoulder. 'Call when you've done and I'll bring you something dry to put on; then it's bed for the rest of the day— and no arguments either!'

But he didn't wait until she had finished a futile search in his bedroom for pyjamas, a nightshirt, anything she could insist that he wear over a near-nakedness that she found impossibly disturbing. With the towel wrapped around his narrow waist, he padded into the room behind her, giving her a frightful start.

'What are you doing?' she cried, unable to keep from staring. 'Couldn't you wait until I'd found your robe or pyjamas?'

'Not very likely, since I don't own either one,' he grinned, but it was a weak, shaky grin that revealed only his weariness. 'As for what I'm doing, I'm doing what you said—going to bed,' he concluded. And before she could say a word he had fumbled his way to the bedside, dropped the towel and scrambled beneath the sheets.

'Can you put some cream or something on the back of my neck?' he asked. 'It hurts like hell.'

'Well, I'm not surprised,' she replied, her own heart racing at the unexpected proximity. It took her a minute to find some sunburn cream, and when she returned he was almost asleep.

Almost . . . not quite. At the touch of her fingers, he first flinched, then seemed to go completely boneless, relaxing as she soothed the cream into his neck, his shoulders, and the angry red upper portions of his arms.

'Turn over and I'll do your face as well,' she said quietly. 'It'll make an unholy mess of the bed-linen, but that doesn't matter now.'

He only grunted, rolling over and lying quietly while she applied the cream first to his face, then his upper chest and down the long red V where his shirt had been open.

'Now go to sleep,' she said—only to have him reach out and grip her wrist in a trembling hand.

'First you have to promise you won't go,' he said, 'that you'll be here when I wake up again.'

'I . . . I . . . promise,' she said. What else could she do in any event? He couldn't be left alone, not with the possibility that he'd got even more sun than she had originally feared. She would have to check him again in an hour, ensure that he wasn't drifting into the far more serious effects of sun-stroke.

'Good,' he said muzzily. 'I . . . rather like the idea of having you here.' And he slipped away almost immediately into a deep-breathing sleep, his fingers still locked around her wrist.

Rena eased herself down to sit on the bed beside him, not pulling away, but letting him slide deeper into his much-needed sleep with her wrist inside the curve of his fingers. Only when he released her of his own accord did she slowly, quietly get up and leave the room.

It took her only a few minutes to slip upstairs to her own flat and change into dry clothing, but throughout she kept her ears cocked for any sound from below.

When she returned, wearing a light T-shirt and shorts and with her hair caught up in a ponytail, Ran lay as she had left him, his breathing deep and slow. She didn't need the thermometer to show her that his temperature had stabilised close to normal.

Imprisoned by her already-regretted promise to stay with him, Rena spent the next hour puttering about the flat, tidying and dusting and marvelling at how little of himself Ran had brought to Queensland.

Except for his clothing and the small cassette player with his favourite tapes, he had brought nothing, it seemed. The flat, of course, had come furnished, but somehow it was . . . sterile, impersonal.

She made herself some coffee, snooped in the fridge to find out what he had been living on, and immediately wished she hadn't. Except for some cheese and fruit it was empty, and the freezer section held only a broad selection of quick-and-easy one-pot meals. Acceptable, she thought, only because even a blind person could manage to fill a pot with water, add the frozen packet and wait for it to boil. But how . . . how horribly isolated!

Rena had been on her own long enough to know the difficulties of cooking for one, how easy it was to simply ignore cooking altogether, to either eat out or do without, simply to avoid the hassles of eating alone and lonely. Being a fairly self-contained person, she coped well enough, but to have to cope—as Ran did—without even seeing . . . the thought shook her.

She drank her coffee, prowled the flat, made another cup, prowled some more, and wondered how he had survived the boredom, much less the blindness.

Despite the stimulative effects of the coffee, Rena found herself becoming sleepy, which wasn't surprising after the day she had had. She thought first of retreating to her own flat, then shrugged off the urge and instead sprawled out on the sofa, where she fell asleep within minutes.

Wakefulness came less easy, but it was spurred by a weak and rather plaintive cry from the bedroom where Ran was resting. Bleary-eyed, Rena swung to her feet and entered the room, only to find that instead of sleeping, he was lying with the covers snugged up to his throat and obviously shivering.

'You said you'd stay,' he said accusingly.

'Well, I did; I was just in the lounge room,' Rena replied. 'What's the matter?'

'I'm cold. Can't stop . . . shivering,' he replied.

'Are there any more blankets?' she asked, already flinging open closet doors in search of some.

'How the hell should I know?' he replied shakily. And how indeed? she thought. If there were any spares, she also couldn't find them.

'I'm sorry . . . would you like something hot to drink?' she asked at the end of the fruitless search. She bent down to touch his forehead, half surprised to find that he didn't feel cold at all. If anything, it was the opposite; his forehead was clammy, but warmer than it should have been.

'I . . . I just want to be warm,' he replied, one hand going up to grasp fumblingly for her wrist. And before Rena could object he had pulled her down against him on the bed.

'You're nice and warm,' he said accusingly. 'Come and lie beside me.'

She flinched away instinctively. Didn't he realise what he was saying? What he was asking—demanding? 'I . . . I . . .' she stammered, trying to free herself but having trouble because now both his arms were around her.

'Oh, don't be such a priss,' he snarled in her ear. 'I'm not going to assault you . . . I just want to . . . to be warm.' And after a few seconds in which she fought a losing battle with her common sense, 'I'll be good—I promise.'

This is madness, she thought, feeling her own body react to his touch, to the feel of his long legs against hers, the firmness of his chest against her breasts, the touch of his muscular back beneath her fingers. Her entire body was alive, alert, poised to repel—or was it to accept?—his advances.

Only there were none. After a moment of shifting around, arranging himself so that he could gain as much of her body warmth as possible, Ran whispered, 'Yes, that's better,' and as his shivering gradually slowed, his breathing did likewise. Within three minutes, he was asleep.

Rena, too, drifted into an uneasy slumber not long afterwards. Only her sleep was punctuated by vivid dreams that kept kicking her towards wakefulness.

The final one was the worst, because it was so vivid, so tangibly real. And because it was the one that merged into reality with a clarity that was frightening.

Rena dreamed of her final night with Ran, the night he had not only slept with her, but had taken from her the most cherished gift she could provide. There had been two other occasions during their whirlwind courtship on which they had slept together, at least after a fashion, but on both those occasions he had insisted on observing convention. He had kissed her, of course, even touched her, but he had used his magnetic, dominant personality to hold them back from that final commitment.

On the last night it had been different. Ran had

known he would be going off to New Zealand to check
out the ugly ramifications of the Springbok Tour. Only
for two days, but they would be the first days he and
Rena had been parted since their romance began.

He had taken her to dinner, choosing the intimacy
of La Potinière, on the North Shore, and then they
had walked and talked into the small hours of the
morning, ending up at Rena's flat about two o'clock.

She had given him his medallion during dinner,
choosing the more public choice of circumstances because it was the first time she had ever bought such an
intimate present for a man, and she had felt vaguely
selfconscious about it. Ran, at the time, had seemed to
suffer no such problem.

'I shall wear it always,' he had promised in his low,
vibrant voice. It wasn't until later, back in her flat,
that he had added the final touch of perfection, promising to think of the medallion as an engagement ring,
promising to hurry up the jeweller who was already
making Rena's engagement ring.

'Diamonds and sapphires,' he had whispered into
her naïve, willing ear. 'The diamonds for tradition,
because I love you and you make me feel traditional,
and the sapphires because they're your birthstone.'

It was enough, for Rena. When he kissed her, gath-
ering her into his arms as they sat together on the
lounge suite, she threw aside all her inhibitions, all her
fears. All that mattered was being in his arms, being
with him, being part of him.

It had been she who had shifted to ease the path of
his light, probing fingers down her throat, into the
hollows of her bare shoulder, and gradually lower until
his palm cupped her breast, the nipple firm and erect
against his love-line.

'God, but you're beautiful,' he'd whispered, then
returned his lips to hers before she could answer,

drinking in the taste of them, sharing it.

The dress she was wearing was nothing special, except in the loose, off-the-shoulder design and the pale cream colour that so well suited her tan. Nothing special until Ran's skilled fingers shifted it lower, baring her breasts to his fingers, to his lips.

He had kissed each of them in turn, then returned to claim her lips with increased desire. His fingers were like live things as they stroked her body, bringing up each nerve, each flame of desire with an expert touch.

'I love you, Catherine,' he had said. For the first time, the most important time. Her heart had threatened to burst, to simply swell up and overflow with the love and the need inside her.

Her fingers had slid from behind his neck to begin an exploration of their own, down along the chain of the medallion, down through the crisp curls to where the silver wafer nestled over the thudding rhythm of his heart. And then lower, unbuttoning his shirt as she went, until her fingers had reached his belt, feeling the muscles of his chest and stomach, the vibrant masculinity of his body.

When he had lifted her, easing the dress from her in a single, practiced motion, she had merely wrapped her arms around his neck and fastened her lips to his while he carried her the short distance to the bedroom and the broad softness of her bed.

'You're sure?' His voice had been a whisper, not really cautioning, but not pleading, either. Merely checking, ensuring that he wasn't pushing her beyond the limits of her own conscience, her own innocence.

'I'm sure,' she had whispered back. 'I love you too.' And she had been sure, as sure as life itself, as sure as her own first poignant love, her raging need for him.

Somehow in the next few moments they both discarded the rest of their clothing, giving each of them

the freedom of true exploration. Ran's fingers and lips
flowed across her body so gently, so exquisitely. It was
like lying beneath a warm shower, being touched
everywhere by light caresses.

So experienced, yet so gentle. He fitted them together, let her set the pace without giving her time to
think consciously about doing so, letting her body take
control, her sensations and her own personal rhythm
create the melody of them together.

She had kissed him, her lips moving slowly across
his mouth, down to his throat, again following the
chain of the medallion. Her fingers had moved even
lower, seeking the essence of him, trembling with anti-
cipation and need, but not fear. She had nothing to
fear from Ran, who loved her.

And then Rena was bolt upright, her eyes widening
as she looked first at her still-trembling fingers and
then at the dark-haired figure beside her. She could
feel the imprint of his hands on her, the touch of his
lips, the smooth, pliant touch of his skin against hers.

'My God!' she cried, struggling against his grasp,
yet unable to deny the willing compliance of her body.

His fingers closed on her wrist, pulling her down
against him so that her bared breasts were firm against
the muscled fur of his chest. His lips searched for her,
oblivious to her weak struggles.

'Stop, oh please, stop,' she murmured, then
suddenly realised from his touch that not only were
her breasts bared, but that her shorts also were no
longer a protection against his physical presence.

'Stop! Oh, damn you, you bastard. Stop this!'

He stopped, puzzlement evident on his face. But he
didn't let her go. His eyes, those copper eyes that had
once drunk in her beauty, looked at her, through her,
past her. Seeing nothing.

'What the hell *is* this?' he demanded, his voice ragged

with a passion she could understand only too well. 'Another little game of tease the blind beggar? Well, sorry, Rena, but you started this game, and by God you'll finish it.'

And she was against him again, his strong arms making her protests useless as his mouth claimed hers in a kiss that was both harsh and gentle, provocative, expert. Her lips were parted, her mouth moulded to his with the same perfection as in her dream.

He didn't need to be able to see to trap her wildly waving arms, in a single motion he folded his own arms around her and shifted so that his weight helped hold her down, one of his legs firm over her own, like an anchor.

His mouth was alive, searching for her reactions, plundering her needs, firing the furnace of desire that flared at his every kiss, his very touch. And in a moment her struggles ceased with the betrayal of her body as it felt his warmth.

'My God, but I want you ... need you,' his voice whispered, a siren song of pure delight in her ear. His lips fled across her cheek, down the long column of her throat, rousing her breasts to new awareness with their touch.

'Oh, Ran ...' She could say nothing more, dared not, lest her mouth also betray her. Her fingers tangled in the hair at the back of his neck, tangled in the chain of the medallion.

She wanted him, at least as much as he wanted her. More, she thought, because she knew exactly what her wanting might lead to. Physical gratification, a renewal of the hunger he had created in her that first time, so very, very long ago. And then? And then only sorrow, only the slow starvation of her heart, because she couldn't keep him; he belonged to someone else and he'd even admitted it to her.

No, it simply couldn't be. And his fingers were playing along the dimples of her spine, expertly creating a tune of such promise that Rena shuddered beneath his touch.

It would be masochism. And his hands moved lower, drawing her close against him, pressing her softness against the rigidity of his masculinity.

It must *not* be! And she shrugged violently, shoving against his chest, kicking her long legs as she fought against the pressure of his arms, against the stronger pressure of her own desire.

'No! No, Ran . . . we can't. Please! No . . . no . . . no . . . no . . .!' She screamed it, over and over and over as she fought him.

'Yes . . . yes . . . yes . . .' His voice mimicked her panic, but he wasn't panicked. He was simply using his superior strength, his vast experience, to shift her again to his side.

Rena got both hands against his chest, pushed with all her strength. Ran laughed, holding her easily. Damn him! If he could see, if he could know it was *her* . . . She shrieked, anger now rising to conquer lust inside her.

'No!' And her fingers reached back to claw at him, only to be restrained by their tangle within the chain of the silver medallion.

Rena yanked, and the chain snapped, flying towards her like a streak of lightning. Damned, hateful, reminder of her own gullibility . . . of Ran's deceit!

She flung it at him, crying a bitter oath as it struck him in the face—cried another as she began to flail about with her fists, now striking his shoulder, his chest, and then his face, his head.

It was working; Ran showed confusion now, uncertainty. She kicked out, scrambling with every muscle in her body until finally she rolled free of the bed, landing hard on the bedside rug with her half-discarded shorts threatening to trip her as she tried to stand . . . to run.

'Damn you!' His voice was a growl of sheer torture, of a beast tormented, tortured beyond control. He reached out blindly, fingers clamping like a vice on her wrist.

'Damn *you*!' she screamed in return, kicking out at him, pulling to free herself and almost falling when Ran, too, tumbled from the bed.

She saw the impact, heard the impact as he fell blindly, head-first, landing in a crumpled heap of naked limbs and tangled bedlinen, but hitting the floor so hard she felt the impact through its vibrations.

But she was free! She scrambled to her feet, tugging at her clothing and scrabbling like a crab to reach the doorway. Behind her, Ran's muffled oaths testified to the fact that he couldn't be badly hurt.

Rena fled. Driven by panic and sheer self-preservation, she ran for the front door of the flat, her ears like those of a hunted doe, picking up the sound as he struggled to follow.

Outside, across the verandah, then up the stairs to her own flat with only a fleeting wonder that it was already falling dark. Inside, she slammed the door and locked it, wishing out loud for an old-fashioned drawbolt. Then she ran quickly to slam the sliding glass doors and lock them as well, feeling horribly vulnerable even then because of all the window space.

And finally she fled to the questionable sanctuary of her own bedroom, where at last tears came to wash down her terror, dilute it, make sense of it.

'My God!' she whimpered into her pillow. Of all the things she could possibly have done . . . surely to torment a blind man—to torment Ran—in such a way must be the worst.

Revenge. Deep within her, the voice seemed to cry like a doom-seeker. Yes, she thought. Revenge! Indeed, she had gained her revenge, leading Ran Logan to a personal, emotional crisis and then dumping him . . . as he had abandoned her. It was even perhaps fitting that she had done it in bed—his bed.

But then why did she feel so horribly wrong about it all? She knew, had known all along, that it was her dream that began today's affair. Not his broken promise, but *her* dream, *her* retrogression into a past best forgotten.

How much better to have simply told him the truth? Even if she had done it that first night, when they were alone together at the college. She had had the chance, could have made the opportunity. But to tell him now? No . . . it would be too cruel, and she had been cruel enough already.

'Rena!' The voice was followed by a thunderous knock on her door, a knock that sounded as if he was trying to kick the very walls down.

'Go away!' she shouted from the bedroom door, already on her feet and rushing to . . . to what? To barricade herself in even more? Likely, she thought, though she hadn't the vaguest idea how she would accomplish such a thing.

'I want to talk to you.' His voice was lower now; as if he sensed she was there, separated from him only by a few inches of masonry and a suddenly-flimsy piece of plywood.

'There's nothing to be said. Go away. Please . . .' And of it all, she meant the *please* the most. She just couldn't face him again tonight, if ever.

'It's important.'

She could have screamed. Then she did scream, as the hysteria she probably should have felt earlier crawled up from within her shattered emotions.

'No. Go away! Go away . . . go away . . . go away . . . go away . . .!' Over and over, like a broken, scratched, shrieking record. And she, now, was thumping on the locked door between them, her fists beating on it in time to her litany of sobbing, shrieking demands.

'All right . . . all right.' She only barely hard the words over her own cries, didn't believe them at first anyway. But when she paused, he spoke again. 'I'm going. Goodnight.' Hard words, bitterly spoken.

Rena ran to the curtain and peeped out. Yes, he was going, descending the stairs with careful, slow steps. Thank heaven!

She retreated to the interior of her own flat, ears tuned to the curious sound of Ran moving around below her. Not quietly, but slamming himself around; she heard a chair go over, could almost visualise him demolishing the flat in his anger.

And then silence. Silence that lasted for almost half an hour, until a taxi pulled up outside and its driver stepped out to walk to Ran's flat and emerge a moment later, guiding his passenger to the cab and depositing him in the appropriate seat. And a moment later the taxi was gone, leaving Rena finally assured that she was alone, that Ran wouldn't be thundering on her door again *that* night, anyway.

Or would he? Not five minutes had passed since his departure, but Rena felt as if it had been hours. Worse, she suddenly felt . . . knew . . . that he would be back, and that when he came back he would insist on talking to her. No matter if it were midnight, he would!

'And I,' she said to herself, 'can't handle that. Can't . . . and won't.'

That decision made, the next one was easier yet. Within ten minutes she had packed an overnight bag with her working gear for the next day, her performing gear for Monday night's gig at the pub. And her guitar.

Within fifteen minutes she was in her car and headed for town.

'And *that* for you, Ran Logan!' she had cried upon leaving the driveway and giving an insolent salute to Ran's non-existent presence. He was more than capable of looking after himself, Rena thought. If anything, too capable. He could certainly cope without her until late Monday night.

He'd have to; she had no intention of returning to the flat before then. In fact there was a serious question if she would ever return at all, but she knew herself well enough to know that those feelings would gradually fade away.

Rena felt less certain about her feelings for Ran. Those, she knew now, would never fade away. Even if—when—he left her again to return to Sydney, she would love him as deeply as ever. But he must never know.

And it was all her own fault. If only, she thought, she had revealed her true identity that first night, had not let them embark on this voyage of deceit . . .

'But I did,' she muttered to herself. 'And there's no going back. To tell Ran the truth now would be worse than useless. He wouldn't believe a word I said—and I don't blame him a bit.'

Rena conveniently ignored the fact that she, too, had been betrayed. It simply didn't matter any more. She loved Ran no matter what . . . loved him so much she was forced to protect him, now, from the truth.

Her publican employer showed mild surprise at Rena arriving twenty-four hours early for her singing engagement, but neither he nor his friendly wife questioned her request for a room. Even her rather feeble explanation that her flat had just been sprayed for insect pests was kindly accepted, and it wasn't until she was alone in the hotel room that the stupidity of the excuse struck Rena herself.

'On a Sunday?' she asked the wan figure in the mirror. 'They must think I'm daft ... right round the twist!' And she was thankful they were nowhere in evidence when she slipped out later to get some tea.

By morning, her embarrassment had faded sufficiently for her to bid them a good morning on her way out to work, and she got through the day with surprisingly few hassles. She'd still have to face Ran Logan ... probably late that night ... but it no longer held the terrors of the night before.

Her day at work had made the difference, or at least one incident during the day. It was little more than a chance comment by one of the solicitors speaking to a colleague in Rena's hearing.

He had been talking about one aspect of a family law case, and although Rena didn't know the intimate details, his comment so totally fitted her own dilemma that she almost cried out on hearing it.

'I don't know why people bother to lie,' he had said. 'One lie invariably leads to another ... and another, until eventually the whole thing collapses like a house of cards. But the truth, just the simple, plain, unvarnished truth—no matter how bad—seems to last for ever.'

The *truth*. Rena thought about it most of the afternoon, mulling over every aspect of her situation. And by the time she sat down to a lonely counter tea that evening before going on stage, she had decided.

She would tell Ran the truth. *Truth!* It would hurt him, though not as much as the telling would hurt her. But at least they would part with a clear conscience on Rena's own part. And maybe ... just maybe ... she would even find out the real reason for his walking out on her in the first place. Better she should know, than to always wonder if it were another woman, sheer

boredom, or simply the fact that Ran had got what he
was angling for and had immediately lost interest.

She would tell him the truth. And she would do it
tonight, even if it meant knocking on *his* door at midnight to do that.

The decision put her into a much-improved mood.
When it came time to begin her performance, Rena
was cheerful and smiling and . . . just . . . right, somehow. She started on a high note with gay, bright songs
that brought audience participation and kept the mood
of the evening lively.

It became one of those rare evenings when nothing
could go wrong. She never hit a wrong chord, not even
a wrong note. Her voice was strong and her memory
functioned perfectly.

And her audience loved it. The pub was packed
when she started, mostly with people who had come in
for a counter meal and were drawn by the music to
overstay their original intent, but there were a few of
her more faithful fans as well.

The drink flowed, the publican was happy, even
Rena was as happy as she could possibly be under the
circumstances. She was halfway through one of her
own compositions, the one that she had always thought
of as Ran's song, before she even realised what she was
singing. And then it was two-year-old habit that made
her look in the direction where memory said that *he*
would be sitting, encouraging her, loving her.

And he was!

The words choked her! her fingers lost their agility
on the guitar strings. Ran? Here? Rena's mind couldn't
take it in, but instinct saved her performance. Her
fingers picked up the rhythm and her voice once again
took up the words. She sang it right to the end, never
taking her eyes from the tall, lean figure at the corner
table.

He didn't smile; she couldn't see his eyes past the reflective glasses, but there was something . . . an aura about him. As Rena moved into her next number it was as if he were the only person in the room, larger than life, filling the place all by himself.

He was dressed in black, and the sheen of the medallion flashed back to her each time he lifted the glass in his right hand. He was sprawled easily, comfortably, in his chair, sitting as he had always sat when he had listened to her in Sydney.

She could almost, in fact, smell his after-shave, he seemed to loom so large in her eyes. Ran Logan—here! And so the truth was out. No denials now; he might mistake her in any other way through his blindness, but never, Rena knew, could he mistake her singing *his* song.

Suddenly she felt weak, boneless. She thought she would drop the guitar, fall from her high, backless stool like some spineless rag doll. Because he was grinning, and it wasn't a friendly grin. It was the cruel, carnivorous grin of a hungry wolf confronted with dinner.

He reached up to take the sunglasses from his eyes, eyes that in the dim light seemed of a sudden to have life . . . to be horribly, threateningly alive. And looking at her, devouring her. It was too much.

'I . . . I think I'll take a break now,' she said into the microphone. And as she stood up, Ran also rose to his feet. He mouthed a single, silent word, then turned on his heel and strode from the room.

CHAPTER NINE

'*BITCH!*' The word echoed over and over through Rena's barely conscious mind. He might well have screamed it at her, so loudly did it now seem to dominate everything else.

Without her stool, she would have fallen. Her knees seemed to belong to someone else; her head felt light, disembodied. For one brief instant she thought she would faint, but it was a fleeting impression.

He was gone. Had he, in fact, even really been there at all? Or was it some cruel trick of the lighting, of the mood, of the song she had been singing? The questions raced through her mind, but Rena knew the answers only too well. Ran Logan had been there, had listened, had spoken that single, silent condemnation. Her body knew it.

But how? And where had he gone, vanishing into the darkness, into his own medium, after that startling and unexpected appearance?

Rena laid down the guitar, took several deep breaths, then walked slowly towards the corner where he had been sitting. Maybe her eyes had deceived her, she thought. Then she saw the empty glass, the cigarette still smouldering in the ashtray. And the sunglasses!

Almost without thinking, she picked them up, staring at them as if they were something she had never seen before. But why had Ran left them?

Because he didn't need them! The answer lanced into her mind even as memory replayed the picture of him *looking* at her, *seeing* her. Yes! And when he had mouthed his curse upon her and left the pub, he hadn't been moving as a blind man. He had strode through the crowded room and out the door with all the power and grace and arrogance she had come to associate with his tremendous vitality.

Ran could see!

A sudden chill ran through her. For how long had he been able to see? she wondered. Had his entire visit to Bundaberg been no more than a horrible, vindictive charade?

Turning quickly, she flashed one hand at the barmaid in a deliberate 'five minutes' signal, then ran for the door and out into the street, the sunglasses in her hand. No sign of him. Her five minutes stretched to ten as she scoured the immediate vicinity, moving down the empty footpaths as if the devil himself were in pursuit. No Ran. Finally, Rena had to give it up, and she returned to the pub half expecting to find him waiting, laughing at her.

The rest of the evening passed in a blur. She sang, she played her guitar, but it had lost the magic. Her act now was mechanical, her mind far from the smoky, crowded bar. When it was all over, she didn't bother to stay for her customary nightcap, but drove immediately back to the flat and the confrontation she knew must be awaiting her.

The drive home was a nightmare, her arrival nothing more than a total letdown. Throughout the twenty-minute trip she ran over and over the things she would say . . . must say, invented complicated scenarios, tried to visualise what Ran would say. But when she got home he wasn't there, and neither was his great black car.

Rena could scarcely credit it. She drove into the now empty carport, got out of her own vehicle, and looked at the empty space beside her as if expecting the black Jaguar to materialise from nowhere.

Then she calmly walked over to bang on the door of Ran's flat, knowing it was futile but nonetheless compelled to make the gesture.

'It's a trick,' she said aloud. 'He's damned well here—somewhere. He must be!'

But it was no trick. He wasn't in *her* flat, as she had half expected, and he didn't arrive at all during the night despite the fact that she sat up until almost dawn waiting for him.

The next two days were a nightmare. She kept expecting him to turn up at any moment, kept looking for his car, for his familiar figure. All in vain. She slept heavily but badly on Tuesday night, only just got through Wednesday without falling asleep at her desk, and simply collapsed when she got home after work to find he still hadn't turned up.

'Bastard!' she hissed at the empty carport. Rena was now convinced it was some devious plot on Ran's part. He could see; he must know she knew he could see. What was he doing?

She woke at seven, heavy-eyed, slightly disorientated, but immediately certain there was something she should be doing. Class! Of course. Whatever Ran's failings, he would never forget a commitment, and that was one thing he definitely seemed to feel strongly about, his teaching.

But could she go? Could she face him now in the presence of others? She wondered, pondering over it uselessly until she cried out in despair. She must; there wasn't a choice.

By the time she had changed and driven back into town, driving far too fast for safety but unable to shirk off her restless energy, she was still fifteen minutes late for class. But Ran was there! The huge black car squatted against the kerb outside the college staff house.

Rena didn't give herself time to think. That would be deadly, she realised. Instead she leapt from her car and walked quickly, almost running up the narrow steps and into the building.

All eyes were on her as she stepped into the room, but her own eyes were drawn to only one pair, the dark coppery eyes of Ran Logan, who looked at her and *saw* her. And grinned mischievously.

'Well . . . well, here's the heroine now,' he drawled, and the rest of the class erupted in a cacophony of questions and cheers and congratulations that rang like bells in her head.

'I . . . don't understand. . .' she began, only to be interrupted by Ran's stronger, deeper voice.

'I've just been telling them how you were instrumental in my regaining my sight,' he said. But his eyes said something quite different—'play along with this, or else!'

'But how? You never did tell us how?' It was Louise, her splendid body pressed against Ran's, staking a definite, unarguable claim.

He didn't answer immediately, which didn't please old John one bit. 'Yes, for God's sake tell us how,' he demanded. 'You may be a great writer, but you're a lousy storyteller!'

Ran laughed at that, but he made no attempt, Rena noticed, to free himself from the octopus grasp of the redhead.

'She gave me a damn great smack across the head—that's how!' he roared. 'And yes, John, I deserved it, too. Now don't ask me what it did, because I don't know and the doctors don't know any more, quacks that they all are. But it sure as hell did something, because when I got up, I could see.'

'Just like that?' John's question entered Rena's

brain, but it was Ran's answer she was waiting for.

'Not quite that simple. At first it was just sort of a fuzzy light. The quacks say it's because I wasn't focusing properly. But within a few minutes—yes, I could see quite normally.'

Rena couldn't believe this was happening. And yet Ran was here, looking at her, talking to her. It must have happened ... she blushed at the memory and looked away.

'What the hell did you do, Rena? Kick him out of bed?' John's eyes twinkled, but Louise's fairly blazed with envy and jealousy at the question.

Ran, damn his soul, laughed outrageously. 'She'll probably say yes, John,' he interjected before Rena could finds the words to speak. 'But don't believe her, because she's a terrible liar.' And his eyes burned as he stared at her, burned with a passionate intensity Rena couldn't bear to face.

'Anyway,' he said finally, 'that's enough of this; you're here to work, so let's get to it.' And the class, for what it was worth, began. For Rena, it might as well not have been. Her mind was little more than a kaleidoscope of impressions, thoughts, worries.

Had Ran really regained his sight because of her pulling him from the bed? She wanted, desperately, to believe it, and yet it sounded so completely unbelievable that she just couldn't.

And yet he was there ... standing before the class, listening to their questions, answering them, and looking at her! Not once did he take his eyes from her, not even when she refused to meet his gaze, to accept the mocking, mischievous lights she saw in those copper-coloured eyes.

Even when she looked away, she could feel him looking at her, could imagine him stripping away her defences with his eyes, revealing her duplicity, her deceit.

Louise was not amused. She, too, could read the direction of Ran's interest, and when she looked at Rena it was with scorn.

The evening stretched on into infinity. Rena found she couldn't concentrate, didn't care if she did or not. This course wasn't ever going to give her what she so desperately needed. It couldn't, because what she needed now had very little to do with creative writing in any context.

And finally it was over. Ran made his final comments, then toured the room making idle chit-chat with various of his students. Louise followed him like a bloodhound; Rena merely looked for the right moment to make her escape.

Rena thought her time had come when Ran was cornered by his two remaining housewives, both of whom seemed bent on extracting every single detail of his miraculous recovery. Moving slowly, so as to draw no more attention than she must, Rena slipped towards the door and then finally, thankfully, through it.

She reached her vehicle and slid gratefully behind the wheel, only to leap with alarm when her door was suddenly flung open and a hand reached in to grasp her shoulder.

'Going somewhere?' His teeth glinted in the street-light and his smile was sardonic, mocking. 'Why not drive home with me, for a change?'

'I .... I can't just leave Matilda here,' she replied, grabbing at the first excuse that came to mind. Now that her confrontation with Ran seemed imminent, she discovered her fears far outweighed her good intentions.

Ran looked critically at the ancient station sedan, his nose wrinkling in distaste. 'Not if there's any chance the civic beautification committee is likely to come by, that's for sure,' he replied. 'But on the other hand, are you sure it'll make it home?'

His sneering stirred Rena's already defensive anger. How dared he insult her car? 'You've got a helluva nerve!' she snapped. 'I didn't notice you complaining when Matilda was providing for your convenience.'

'That,' he replied, 'was because I couldn't see the heap of junk I was riding in. But please yourself; I didn't come to start an argument.'

'Well, you've a fine way of showing it,' she said. 'I don't know why you bothered to come at all. If you must offer somebody a lift, why not try Louise?' It was catty and childish, and Rena knew it, but she couldn't help herself.

Ran only snorted. 'Credit me with a *little* taste,' he said. 'Shall I put the coffee on while I'm waiting for you at home, then? Or do you reckon a drink would be more in keeping with the occasion?'

'I didn't know there was an occasion,' Rena replied. 'And it's my intention to make an early night of it, if you don't mind.'

'The road to hell is paved with good intentions,' was the enigmatic reply. 'I'll see you there, then.' And he wa gone, closing the door behind him, as if he were afraid that to slam it might cause further problems for the elderly car.

Rena muttered an angry curse as she wheeled the old car around at the first intersection, only too aware that Ran's larger but more modern machine had already done a U-turn and that he was ghosting along the road ahead of her at speeds she dared not try to match. Especially not on the highway, where Matilda tended to shudder and wheeze at anything beyond the legal limit.

Sure enough, he was waiting for her when she arrived, standing on his verandah with hands on his hips and a look of amused expectation on his face. He was there to open the car door for her, too, obviating any ideas she might have of fleeing directly to her own flat.

'Come into my parlour, said the spider to the fly,' he grinned. 'Only stop looking so apprehensive, dear Rena. Or is it Catherine tonight? Just remember that confession is good for the soul.'

Her stomach leaped. So this was to be the way of it, a direct assault laced with mockery and humour . . . or what Ran Logan thought was humour? His hand was on her elbow, gently but firmly insisting that she accompany him.

Once inside, he deposited her in one armchair and her handbag in another, then stepped into the small kitchen and poured each of them a drink without asking if Rena wanted one or not. His eyes, when he handed her the glass, were unreadable but bright with expectation. Then he took his own seat across from her and spoke.

'Here's to being able to see again,' he said, lifting his glass in a toast. 'Now tell me, woman of a thousand names, just what the hell you've been playing at?'

'I haven't been playing at anything,' she retorted. 'It's been . . . anything but a game, I assure you.'

'Humph! Don't bother with assurances; it's explanations I want,' he snorted. 'And you can start with explaining why all this silliness of the secret identity. Surely there must be some sane, logical reason why you couldn't have just told me who you were in the first place.'

'No.'

'No?' His voice hardened angrily. 'For God's sake, woman ... first you run out on me, then when we finally meet again you lie to me, deliberately deceive me ... and you deny there's an explanation?'

'I didn't say that.'

'You damn well did!'

'I didn't. I said there wasn't a sane, logical reason for it. And there wasn't ... my word there wasn't,' she sighed. Then realisation of what he had said seemed to focus in her wildly whirling brain.

'And what the hell do you mean, I ran out on you? I did no such thing, and you very well know it! It was you who ran out on me, once you'd got me into bed and had what you wanted. And don't you dare try to deny that, either!'

'I wouldn't dream of it,' he said wearily. 'But the truth of that can wait. I want to know about why you felt you had to deceive me here ... in Bundaberg ... now.'

'I hated you, that's why!' Rena's fragile control began to slip, then lost any semblance of balance. 'Just how do you think I felt, finding you here of all places? I ... I couldn't believe it, at first. And to find you ... blind ...' she shuddered at the memory of it, then plunged on, recalling all of her feelings, her anger, her confusion.

'So you decided a little revenge was in order.' He grinned. 'My word, it must have given you a helluva shock to have me turn up here in this flat. I'd give a million dollars to have been able to see your face!'

'It's not funny,' Rena cried. 'None of this funny; it's all been nothing but a cruel, horrible ...' She just couldn't go on.

'Oh, what tangled a web we weave ... etcetera,

etcetera,' he crooned sadistically. 'Well, I must admit you got your revenge the other night, although the climax was a bit different from what you expected, I'll bet. Are you satisfied with it, Rena? Or does having given me back my sight take away some of the satisfaction?'

'Oh!' she stuttered, unable to believe the cruelty of his accusation. 'I ... I ... oh, you utter, unspeakable bastard! I was not seeking revenge, and I'm at least as glad as you are about your sight coming back.'

He sat there, grinning at her like the Cheshire Cat and fiddling with the medallion at his throat. 'I could almost believe you,' he said musingly. 'And all of this, then, goes back to the fact that I bedded and abandoned you two years ago, took your innocence and walked away?'

He sighed then, the deep, soul-weary sigh of somebody finally released from bondage. And when he looked up at her, his eyes were no longer mocking, but sad beyond comprehension.

'Ah, Rena,' he said softly, 'sometimes I really wonder how I could be in love with somebody as stupid as you are.' And to her total astonishment, he shrugged. 'But then I've got to be just as stupid, so we're probably well matched.'

Rena couldn't believe her ears. Had Ran really said he was in love with her? Her mouth opened, but no words emerged. Before she could even begin to find the words he had suddenly flung his empty glass across the room and lurched to his feet like a man demented.

'Oh ... God *damn* that bitch Valerie,' he raged. 'I shouldn't have just fired her; I should have broken her bloody lying neck while I was at it!'

Then he looked at where Rena sat, white-faced and

totally confused, unsure that she had heard what she thought she had heard, even less sure she understood it. And his anger flowed away in a visible tide.

He came over to—surprisingly—kneel before her, taking her hands in his. 'Poor Rena,' he said. 'You really don't understand at all, do you?'

She nodded mutely, making no attempt to free herself from his touch. His voice, when he spoke again, was strangely gentle, hauntingly persuasive.

'Tell me what happened—exactly what happened—when I supposedly abandoned you back in Sydney. I think I know, but I'd like to hear your side of it.'

'Does it matter, now?' she asked incredulously. She had no wish to relive those frantic, heartrending days of being put off by Ran's secretary, of demeaning herself.

'It matters more than you can imagine,' Ran replied, rising to seat himself on the arm of her chair with his hand still holding her fingers. 'It matters because when you've told me, my love, I'll explain to you how both of us have spent two long years in the middle of the most vile deception imaginable.'

My love. He'd said it, and Rena could no longer ignore the words. They seemed to pierce like arrows to her troubled heart.

'Why do you call me your love?' she asked. 'I'm not . . . I never was and you know it.'

'You have been since the day I first met you,' he replied. 'Even since the *second* first day that I met you, although all this damned foolishness with names had me fooled for a bit. Ah, Rena, what fools we've both been! It was Valerie who told you it was all off, wasn't it? While I was lying blind in a New Zealand hospital bed and couldn't reach you myself, when I had to trust her . . . fool that I was!'

He rose suddenly and once again stormed around the room, thumping one huge fist into the palm of his other hand as if the sheer physical violence of the act could still his turbulent emotions.

'Wasn't it?' he demanded. 'Just as she lied to me about you, the treacherous bitch! She told me she'd tried to take my messages to you, had tried to find you, but after the first message—the one saying I was blinded in the riot—you'd made it abundantly clear you wouldn't be saddled with a blind man.'

And the penny dropped. Rena realised with startling clarity just what Ran was saying. She started up out of her chair, eyes wide with astonishment.

'Are you really saying what I think you're saying?' she cried. 'That . . . that your secretary lied— deliberately—to *both* of us?' He didn't have to answer; it was there to be seen in his coppery eyes, eyes that now softened with a love Rena could no longer deny.

'My God!' she whispered, flowing into his arms, cherishing the touch of him, the warmth and strength of his arms around her. She shuddered at the horror of what he had said.

'It's true,' he whispered in her ear. 'The bitch deliberately and coldly arranged the whole thing. She lied to me, knowing I couldn't see to do anything about it, and to you because you couldn't fight her either.'

'But . . . but why?' It was a silly question; Rena realised that as soon as she'd asked it. Valerie Dunn had wanted Ran, and indeed she had got him.

'Power? Money? Who knows . . . maybe she just fancied my exquisite body,' he replied in a lame attempt to jest about it. 'What worries me is that she damned near got away with it; you've no idea how much a blind person comes to depend on someone who can see.'

'We've both been blind,' Rena replied, 'and I think me even more than you. Oh, Ran, I'm so sorry. If only I'd trusted you more, if only . . .'

'How could you have trusted me more?' he asked gently. 'You'd only known me for two weeks. God, it must have been unbelievably easy to believe that damned Valerie. It was for me; she made it all seem very, very plausible.'

'Yes, but . . .'

'No buts,' he said, his lips sliding down to claim her mouth in a kiss as soft as butterfly wings. 'Just tell me you love me. That's what I've been wanting to hear.'

'Oh, I do. I do,' she whispered. 'More than anything, more than life itself. That's what makes this all so . . . so awful. I've never stopped loving you. Even when I . . . hated you. And yet I should have trusted you . . . I should have.'

'I think we both have to cop a bit of guilt on that score,' Ran replied, releasing her. Now, how about another drink? There's still a fair bit of explaining to do and I'm suddenly dry as hell.'

He disappeared into the bedroom while Rena mixed their drinks, and once she had finished he reached out for her hand, drawing her against him. 'I do love you,' he said, 'and I do want to marry you.'

And he reached out to place on her finger the largest, most beautiful engagement ring she had ever seen. It was an enormous diamond, surrounded by sparkling sapphires in a setting that had obviously been specially designed and handmade.

Rena gasped. 'It's . . . it's incredible!' she exclaimed. 'But how . . . where . . .' Words failed her; she could only look from the ring to Ran's smiling eyes and back again, her heart fluttering in her breast and tears lurk-ing behind her eyelids.

'Sapphires and diamonds, just as I promised,' he said softly. 'I've been carrying it around with me since ... since the day I got back from Zew Zealand and went looking for you myself, because I just couldn't believe that bitch Valerie wasn't ... mistaken or something.'

There was a catch to his voice, something unsaid that Rena knew must come out, out in the open to be dissembled like all the other misconceptions. And she knew what it was.

'Was that ... when you became blind again?' she asked, almost afraid of the answer. 'Was it? Was it really because of *me*?'

He didn't seem to have heard the question, but stayed looking at her, his fingers again toying with the silver medallion.

'I think that without this I'd have lost my sanity,' he mused. 'I've never taken it off, you know. Not once since you put it there. They wanted to remove it in the hospital, but I taught them a few new words and they left it.'

'Ran ... answer my question,' Rena pleaded. She had to know, no matter how much it hurt.

'It wasn't because of *you*—it was because of that damned lying Valerie,' he replied finally. 'But yes, it started then. It didn't happen all at once; my sight just started to fade out again. I don't know if being told you'd just ... just damned well disappeared is what caused it, even the doctors didn't know. But it was amazingly coincidental, especially in view of how it came back in the end.'

'Was it really because of me dumping you on the floor, or was that just a story you made up?' Rena wanted, really, to forget about that evening, and yet she had to *know*.

Ran shrugged. 'It really was. I landed head-first, and came up with the bedding all over my head. It wasn't until I pulled it off that I realised I could see light again—not much, but definitely light.'

'Is that ... what you were trying to tell me was important?'

'Well, of course. And you, damn you, wouldn't have a bar of it, not that I blame you considering the circumstances. Anyway, I took a cab to the hospital, where I spent the night, and by morning my sight was almost back to normal.'

'I spent the night at the pub,' she said, wondering why that fact should be important under the circumstances.

'So that's why you weren't here when I got back in the morning. I wondered about that,' he said. 'They told me to check with my own doctor, but before I left the hospital I happened to pick up the morning paper. God, you can't imagine how good it was to be able to read a paper again ... or so I thought until I saw the advertisement about your pub performance.'

He grinned, suddenly, an engaging, delighted grin. 'That's what put it all together for me, actually, although I had to see for myself, and once I'd actually seen you I blew my top entirely. If I hadn't left I would have strangled you right on the spot, but on the plane to Sydney I got everything into perspective.'

'I don't understand. You've been to Sydney?'

'Hell, yes! I went directly to the airport from the pub on Monday night. I just got back tonight in time for the class, or I'd have found you wherever you were hiding, you can bet on that. But it was that advertisement, really. When I saw that, I knew damned well somebody was lying—somebody besides *you*, I mean. Because from the very first day we arrived here, I'd specifically asked Valerie to check for anybody singing in pubs. She said there was no one, but of course she knew all along that you were, although I don't think she realised just exactly *who* you were.'

'You ... you actually came to Bundaberg looking for me? After two years?'

'I never stopped looking for you,' he said. And in his eyes was the light of truth, undeniable truth. 'I've spent a fortune on private investigators looking all over Sydney for you, but I didn't remember until just a while ago that you'd mentioned growing up here. When I did remember, I came, much to Valerie's disappointment. Not that I think she expected me to find you; she could ensure that never happened. But she so hated being away from Sydney ... you have no idea how she hated it.'

'It's like some kind of fairy story,' Rena said wonderingly.

'Complete with wicked witch,' he replied, enfolding her in his arms. 'And now that I've found you, I'm never going to let you go again.'

His lips came down on hers like a fairy kiss, so soft, so incredibly gentle, that she could barely feel the pressure. But she could feel the emotion that flowed between them like an electric current, and her own lips parted in response.

The kiss went on for ever, without harshness, without pain, without fear. Ran's arms gradually tightened around her, while her own flowed up around his neck, pulling him closer, slowly increasing the pressure of his mouth.

'God, but I want you,' he whispered when the kiss was done. 'It seems like forever since I've held you like this.'

'It's only been a few days, really,' Rena whispered.

'Yes, but then I couldn't see what I was doing. So that means it doesn't count.' He was teasing now, his lips nibbling at her ear, his fingers gliding enticingly across her breast.

'I didn't notice it slowed you down any,' she replied, her own fingers caressing the nape of his neck, the strong line of his jaw.

'Being blind slowed me down more than you can imagine,' he said. 'It always made me just that little bit unsure, despite knowing it was you . . .'

'How long have you known?' She was pulling back against his arms, now, peering intently into his face. 'And don't lie to me, because I'll know if you do.'

Ran grinned, then bent to kiss the tip of her nose. 'Well,' he said, 'I suspected almost right from the start. Your voice was too familiar, *you* felt too familiar. But I guess I didn't know for certain until the first time I kissed you. After that the problem was trying to figure out what you were up to.'

'That long?' She didn't know whether to be angry or not. 'But that means . . .'

'That I've been playing you like a fish for weeks,' he admitted. 'And fair enough, my love, considering you've been doing very much the same thing.'

'That's no excuse. So you knew, then, when you moved in here?'

'I knew the girl who lived upstairs was named Everett . . . I didn't know it was my own Rena Everett/Catherine Conley until I met you at the bottom of the stairs.'

'But you knew when we went for that walk, and you knew when you were feeding me those lines about being deserted because of your blindness, and all that.'

'Just as you knew damned well who I was when you

were feeding me those lines about being bedded and abandoned,' he replied, 'so that makes us even, I reckon.'

'It makes you a cunning, devious man,' Rena growled, feigning a toothy bite at his throat.

'It does. And I'd say we're well matched, my love,' Ran replied, 'so we'll have to get married—it wouldn't be fair to saddle anybody else with either one of us.'

'I'm not sure I want to marry anybody who goes to such lengths to make me jealous,' Rena whispered, her fingers making their own music in the hair of his chest. 'And you did, didn't you? With Louise ... and even that night with Valerie?'

'Of course, but don't ever mention that bitch's name in my presence again,' he said.

'Which bitch?' His shirt was open to the waist now, but he couldn't have noticed because his own fingers were as busy as her own.

'You know very well which bitch,' he scoffed. 'Louise was only ever, if you'll pardon the expression, a red herring.'

Rena laughed. 'I was ... going to tell you—to confess, I mean—when I got home on Monday night,' she said. 'A bit late, considering you obviously knew already. I've ... wanted to all along, but once I'd got started lying, I just didn't dare. I was too afraid of hurting you, especially after what you'd told me about the girl who deserted you.'

'And I hoped I'd be able to provoke the truth out of you during our walk on the beach,' he said. 'Damned near did, too, didn't I?'

'I'm not admitting anything,' she replied. 'And stop that, unless you want this conversation to change venues.'

Ran didn't stop. 'Of course I do,' he whispered, his

hands constantly adding new delight as her clothing fell away. 'Only I'm not afraid to admit it.'

'Neither am I,' Rena whispered as he lifted her in his arms and walked towards the bedroom door. 'Neither am I.'